At the Turn of the Hour

By G. H. Teed

Illustrated by Val Reading

First published in the Union Jack magazine,
Series 2, No. 639; 8 January, 1916.

Stillwoods Edition

Stillwoods.Blogspot.Ca

Catalogue Information:
Title: At the Turn of the Hour
Author: G. H. Teed (1881-1938)
Illustrated by: Val Reading
First published anonymously in the Union Jack magazine, Series 2, No. 639, 8 January, 1916.
This Edition by: Stillwoods, 2021
ISBN Canada: 978-1-989788-79-0
Blog: Stillwoods.Blogspot.Ca
Author Blog: http://ghteed.blogspot.com/
Storefront: http://www.lulu.com/spotlight/lulubook22

https://tinyurl.com/ve25d42s This link should go to a spreadsheet of all known Teed stories. The list is annotated with various information on the stories and my progress with recapturing the work. The library of Teed's stories increases almost weekly. Check at the **Lulu.Com** for the latest arrivals. Search for Teed./drf

Keywords: Sexton Blake, British fictional detective, Tinker, Yvonne Cartier, Quebec City

Cautionary Note: This series of books by Stillwoods are intended to make the stories of G. H. Teed, born in New Brunswick, Canada, available to collectors and researchers. The editor, or rather digitizer has not altered the original publication.

This story may contain language and racial terms that are not appropriate to today. I apologize for them; I know that the author was using his voice to excite and entertain an adventurous English audience. These works were published from 82 to 110 years ago. Most every work has characters of redeeming ethnicity within.

I hope you enjoy and share these stories; I have.
Doug Frizzle

A Magnificent, Long, Complete Story of Detective Work and Thrilling Adventure introducing Sexton Blake, Detective, Tinker, Yvonne, and The Island of Mystery.

Specially Written for this issue of the UNION JACK by the Author of "The Man With The Scarred Throat," "Fugitives From Justice" &c.

/drf – Should have read "The Man with The Scarred Neck"

Intercolonial Railway along St. Lawrence River   /drf

Fenwick then turned to the girl, and Tinker saw her go unashamedly into his arms.

The First Chapter.   A Powerful Plea—At the Turn of the Hour— Love's Victory.

"YOU have not told me the truth. No man ever wore that look on his face unless he were in fear."

The low, clear tones of the speaker penetrated to every corner of the room, and the man to whom they were spoken shifted uneasily in his chair.

It was not a sumptuously-furnished room in which the girl and the man sat. Rather did it present to the critical eye the bravely-flaunted front of an attempt to make much of little.

It was the one "reception-room" of a small flat in a mean block of mansions in Earl's Court, and the few articles of cheap furniture revealed the spectre of genteel poverty which crouched behind—a spectre than which there is none more terrible.

The girl who had spoken with such trenchant vehemence was sitting on a chintz-covered window-seat, while the man to whom the words had been addressed, slouched in a chair close to her.

The girl was like a rare flower cast among the mean stubble of the field, so softly toned was her colouring and so graceful her bearing in that poor abode. She held her head proudly, for all the tawdry cheapness about her, and as she swayed gently where she sat her lithe young body bent with supple grace.

She was a very beautiful girl, and the long hours behind the counter of a great department-store had not yet chased the bloom of lovely youth from her cheeks.

Her story was a brief and sad one. The daughter of gentlefolk, she had been born in the country, and until two years before the opening of this story, had known nought but the influence of a cultured and happy home.

Then, with the suddenness with which Fate strikes, came blow after blow. The father, who had stood as a rock between her and the world, was found crouching over the desk in his study with a heavy-calibred revolver beside him, and one of the chambers empty.

Hot on this had come the revelation of Fate's malice. Her father had been ruined. Every penny was gone. The home which had been theirs was suddenly invaded by men who thrust them out into a strange and heartless world.

All their worldly goods were sold to pay debts of which they knew nothing, and with souls still numb from the effects of the blows they had received, mother and daughter had sought for some path to follow.

Like a good many before them, their eyes had turned to London. Surely in that great city they would find the explanation, and the delivery they sought. The mother could do nothing, but the daughter could try writing, and so, with the flame of hope again burning in their breasts, they had journeyed to town.

Most of their small hoard went in furnishing the tiny flat in Earl's Court, and then the girl had tried her hand at writing. It was not for want of trying that she did not succeed.

Night after night the midnight-oil was burned, and post after post carried away the finely-written manuscript with her name and address in the lower right-hand corner. Just as regularly as they went out on their silent plea, just so regularly did they come back with "the editor's regrets."

It seemed so easy to write. She had felt sure that she could do it. But, alas! she had not learned that great lesson which those who write must imbibe. She had not learned that one cannot write unless one has something to write about.

Many are the wrecks strewn about the path which leads to editorial acceptance. Many are the haggard faces one sees on that difficult ladder of achievement.

Nancy Fordyce could not write that which she had not experienced. An uneventful life behind her—an utter and abysmal ignorance of the lurking sorrow of life, with the exception of her one poor little sorrow, which, after all, is the lot of many—gave her but an empty well to draw from.

The spirit of inspiration might send her to the well with the bucket, but if the well contained no water then must she return with the bucket empty.

So it had gone on month after month, until the regularity of the plunk of the returned manuscripts in the letter-box was only equalled by the persistent shrinkage of their small stock of money.

Finally, the day had come when Nancy had been forced to put away her paper and pens, and to seek work which would bring in a certain and regular wage. In a large department-shop in Oxford Street she had found a place, and though the wage was small indeed, it served to keep the tiny home together; and, sailing on the flood-tide of the river of experience, Nancy hoped to gather sufficient material to write something which would receive the sympathetic consideration of an editor.

Then into her life had come that experience which develops a woman as nothing can. Love had sought her out. Wilbur Fenwick and Nancy Fordyce had met some twelve months before.

Fenwick was employed in one of the big banks in the City, and the fact that he was rapidly raised from one post of responsibility to another even greater was proof sufficient that his services were appreciated by his employers.

For a young man still under thirty he had done well indeed, and that Nancy Fordyee was not already his wife was her own fault.

Twelve months of palpitating joy it had been, with the girl revelling in the sweetness of the happiness which loomed so close before her, and which promised recompense for the suffering of the past two years.

It meant a home—it meant the fulfilment of the love which sang within her—it meant all that love can mean.

Nor did she forget the while she sighed happily that it meant a surcease of care for the little mother who had borne up so bravely.

But only a short week ago an insidious reptile of fear had eaten into her life. From a gay and laughing young man Wilbur Fenwick had changed to a taciturn and distraught old man.

The wine of youth seemed departed from his blood. His eyes lost the sparkle born of good spirits and honest endeavour. His shoulders had acquired a stoop, and his face appeared lined and haggard. It was the flag flaunted by a harried soul.

Overwork had been his explanation to the worried inquiries of his fiancee, and for a time that had done. But as his harried look deepened, as he became nervous and jumpy at the slightest sound, the clear eyes of the girl had searched him deeply; and now on this evening when they sat in the poor little reception-room of the flat in Earl's Court, she had challenged him in no uncertain manner.

There was something in the hunted look of her lover which reminded her vaguely of the expression which had rested in her father's eyes just before they had found him lying across his desk, and with a desperate fear biting at her soul, she had determined on knowing the truth.

If she had lacked the experience of the depths of human sorrow,

Nancy Fordyce was to get it and to spare.

"You have not told me the truth," she repeated tensely. "It won't do, Wilbur. It is not overwork, as you say, which is causing you to change so. I, too, work hard, but it has not given me the look which you wear. You are in a responsible position at the bank, and when you come to me with such a look in your eyes it makes me afraid. Nor is it fair of you to leave me in the dark. We start poorly indeed when we start with concealment. Are things bad at the bank? Are you worried over your position? If so, tell me. I am not afraid of the truth. It is only concealment which makes me fear. What is it? I know the explanation is not only overwork."

Fenwick's head was bent, and his eyes were hidden from the girl while she spoke. Had she seen them then her worst fears would have been realised, for cringing fear lay exposed in them. It were strange indeed if the psychical power of her love had not felt the demon which lurked behind.

Fenwick did not reply at once. Indeed, he seemed not to have heard her plea, so still was she; but suddenly from between his hands his voice sounded hoarse and strained.

"It is useless for me to keep things from you any longer, Nancy," he said thickly. "I have tried to do so, but it must come out some time. Yet I do not know how I can tell you. It will make you despise me, and—and I couldn't bear that."

The girl was on her feet in an instant, then she had dropped on her knees beside him.

"What do you mean, Wilbur?" she asked, in a voice laden with fear. "What do you mean? Speak out at once. Can you not see the awful suspense in which I am? Have you done something wrong?"

"Heaven help me, but I have!" he replied. "Oh, Nancy, how can I tell you?"

"Is this the love you boasted of?" she asked scornfully. "Is this the proof of your promise to me? Does it amuse you to come here and to frighten me so? Can you not see that I am at the fag-end of my self-control? If you do not tell me what is the trouble, I shall not be accountable for what I do? It is something terrible I know, but whatever it is, tell me. I am not such a weak creature that things should be hidden from me. Besides, what affects you affects me. If you are in trouble, I shall do all in my power to help you. But if you have done wrong, don't add to it by being a coward. Come, Wilbur, speak out!"

He shot out one hand, and gripped her shoulder.

"I will speak out!" he panted. "I will speak out, and I will tell you everything! Listen!"

He paused for a single instant, during which the girl on her knees heard the ticking of the clock on the mantelpiece. Then the sound of his voice came again, and as he proceeded with his confession, not sparing himself, it must be confessed, the girl's heart froze within her.

"Nancy," he said thickly, "I have been a fool. You know how hard I have worked during the last five years, and you know how quickly I have been advanced at the bank. It is only six months since they put me in charge of all the foreign exchange, as you know I had the handling of very large sums of money in that department, Nancy, but I swear to you that until two weeks ago the money meant nothing to me. It was merely so much material that must be received or paid out or checked. I never felt personally identified with it. Very few bankers do, as they can tell you.

"Moreover, there is no excuse for what I did. I was well paid, and I was saving money. Then, Nancy, in an evil moment, I did a mad thing. You know that I put some money in a tropical estates company. It looked so promising that I put in more than I should.

"Well, about three weeks ago, things began to go badly with the company, and a meeting of the shareholders was held. I attended it, and it was decided to change the board of directors, and to make a further call on all the shareholders for ten shillings on each share. That call came to me just a week before my salary was due. I had no money ready at the time, and, wishing to meet the amount, I—I borrowed from the bank without their knowledge.

"Listen while I explain. As I have just told you, I handled all the foreign exchange business. The firm does a big business with South America, and on the day I needed the money to meet the call on the shares, there was among the drafts one for exactly the sum I needed.

"I decided to use that draft, putting it through another bank for the purpose, and since I was authorised to sign such documents, it was easy enough. I cashed it as I had planned, and used the money to meet the shares. My salary would be paid to me in a week, and it was my intention to collect the draft and repay it into the bank.

"In that way the thing would have been covered up, and no one would have been the wiser. But I counted without considering the man on whom the draft was made might tumble to what had been done. That would have been impossible had it not been that he happened to have an account at the very bank through which I passed the draft.

"Two days after I paid the call on the shares a man came into the bank where I am employed, and asked to see the foreign exchange clerk. He was shown into my room, and introduced himself as Baron Robert de Beauremon.

"Thinking he wished to see me about a foreign draft, I received him; but when the door was closed, he came close to the desk, and spoke to me about the draft I had put through the other bank! 'That draft was on me,' he said, 'and I should like to know what you mean by putting it through the P— Bank on your own signature, when I especially requested that it come through Prout, Green & Co.' — which is my bank, as you know, Nancy.

"What could I say? He had discovered what I thought would never be discovered. It was his own draft which I had used. He knew that I had no business putting it through the P— Bank, and had me at his mercy. I thought, of course, that he would go at once to the principals and tell them what I had done.

"In hopes that he might give me a chance to fix things up, I told him everything. He listened, and then, when I had finished, he said: 'Well, Mr. Fenwick, I have heard your story, and I have no doubt you acted with no intent to defraud your firm. Yet the fact remains that you have used their money for your own purposes, and, if it were discovered, you would be arrested at once. Now I know what has happened, because it is my own draft which you used. When that draft was presented to me for my acceptance by the P— Bank, I knew in a moment that something was wrong. It should have been presented by Prout, Green & Co. I saw that it had been put through the P— Bank by one Wilbur Fenwick, and it did not take me long to discover that Wilbur Fenwick was the foreign exchange clerk of Prout, Green & Co. It looked fishy to me, Mr. Fenwick, so I called to talk it over quietly with you. Now you have confessed what you have done, I understand what before I only suspected. I shall have to think things over, Mr. Fenwick, and in a day or two I shall tell you what I intend doing in the matter'."

Fenwick broke off here, and dropped his head still lower. The girl was on her knees, her body rigid, and her face tense. Her eyes were closed, and she made no attempt to interrupt him.

After a few moments he continued:

"I am telling you everything just as it happened. I have repeated the interview word for word. Two days passed, and I was in a fever of suspense. I did not know what this man Beauremon would do. I expected every day to be called into the chief's office and accused of the thing.

"But at the end of the second day a note was sent to the bank to me. It was from this man Beauremon, and in it he requested me to meet him at the Hotel Venetia that same evening. If you will remember, it was the evening we were to go to the theatre, and I had to ask you to let me off. I told you it was a business appointment, but, Heaven help me, I did not tell you what sort of business!

"Well, I went and had dinner with Beauremon. He kept me on tenterhooks all through the meal, for he did not mention the matter at all. After dinner we went out to the lounge for coffee, and there he brought it up. Oh, that I had gone straight to Mr. Prout or Mr. Green, and confessed all before I listened to this man Beauremon! But I was in deadly fear lest he gave me away, and he knew it.

"Well, Nancy, the long and short of the matter is that he put before me a proposition whereby I was to get possession of upwards of fifty thousand pounds' worth of foreign drafts, which I was to put through the P— Bank on my signature, as I had put his through.

"Of course I refused, but he only laughed. 'Then', he said, if I did not do it he would go to the firm and tell them what I had done. I was between the devil and the deep sea, and they would not believe me if I had told them in turn that he had tried to force me to rob them of fifty thousand pounds. Still I hung out, but it didn't seem to affect him at all.

"While we were sitting there, another man joined us. Beauremon introduced him as Duke Paul Servitch. I don't know anything about him, but he was on very intimate terms with Beauremon. He sat down, and the first thing Beauremon did was to tell this man, Duke Paul Servitch, what I had done. Then he outlined his plan to me. It had been carefully thought out, and I knew it could be brought off easily enough. But for such an amount it was risky, and discovery was bound to follow very soon.

"Whichever way it went, it meant ruin to me as far as I could see it. But Beauremon said it didn't. He said he would so arrange things that suspicion would be cast elsewhere. To do that, he was to make a draught against the P— Bank for fifty thousand pounds, requesting that it be collected through Prout, Green & Co.

"In that way the drafts I put through the P— Bank would balance the draft he made on us. Then he was to default in the payment of his draft, and maintained that, in the fuss which would follow, I could save myself by saying that I had put the fifty thousand pounds' worth of drafts through the P— Bank to meet the fifty thousand pound draft on us.

"On the face of it the scheme looked feasible enough, but I would not consent to have anything to do with it. The upshot was we parted without my knowing what my fate would be.

"I heard nothing the next morning, but just after lunch a note was handed in to me from Beauremon. In it he said that he had made a draft for fifty thousand pounds on Prout, Green & Co., and that it would come through the P— Bank.

"He ordered me to take good drafts to that amount from the foreign exchange department, and to put them through the P— Bank. I was to collect the money for them, and then meet him and hand it over to him.

"If I did so, he guaranteed to keep silent about what I had done, and said that if anything came out, as of course it must when he dishonoured his draft, that all the blame would fall on him, and that it didn't matter, for he would be far away by then.

"I stalled things off for another day, but the next morning his draft was handed in by a messenger from the P— Bank, and—and, Nancy. I put it through the account. That was the day before yesterday. That afternoon I myself went to the P— Bank and drew the cash against the draft. Beauremon knew I had done so, and he immediately sent a note telling me to bring the money to the Hotel Venetia the night before last.

"I did not—I could not. He telephoned me yesterday to take it last night, threatening me with exposure if I did not do his bidding. I put him off some way, and let him think I would go. I was trying desperately to think up some plan to get out of the predicament.

"And now to-day he has called me up again. He says if I do not go to the Hotel Venetia before eleven-thirty this evening he will post an anonymous letter to the bank, telling them what I have done. He says he has it already written out, and I believe him.

"That is the story of what a fool I have been, Nancy. Whatever happens now I am ruined—I, who had worked so hard and had such hopes. I have been mad—mad, Nancy! You will despise me, and I shall deserve the worst you can think of me. I have tried time and again to confess this to you, but I could not bring myself to do it. That—that is all."

Nancy Fordyce got to her feet and began pacing up and down the room. For five or six minutes she walked like a caged tiger, her brow wrinkled in thought. Finally she stopped before her lover's chair.

"This money which you say you got at the bank, and which you are supposed to take to Beauremon to-night—where is it?" she asked.

"In my pocket," replied Fenwick.

"Let me see it," she demanded.

Mechanically he thrust his hand in his pocket and drew out a great pile of banknotes.

As she took them with a shudder she ran her fingers through them quickly, then looked down at him.

"These notes are all foreign notes," she said. "Why is that?"

"I got them that way to prevent them being traced by the numbers," he replied. "If they had been English notes, it would have been a simple matter to trace them."

"You did all you could to protect yourself," she remarked bitterly. "How much is in this pile?"

"Between forty-nine thousand and fifty thousand pounds."

With a quick gesture Nancy thrust the whole pile inside her blouse.

Fenwick, seeing the action, half started up.

"What are you doing, Nancy?" he asked.

"I am taking care of these notes for the present," she replied quietly. "What I do with them afterwards all depends on what arrangement we arrive at. You have been a fool, Wilbur—an awful fool. I did not think you could have made such a hash of things. For the sake of a temporary convenience you have got yourself into a position where you stand a chance of going to prison. If I did not love you, and if I did not think that you had been more of a fool than a knave, I should put you from my mind. But it happens that I do love you. I gave you all the love of my nature, and I did not give it to you to take away at the first trouble which arose. I do not know if you still wish my love, but if you do, then we must think up some plan without delay whereby we can find a way out of the difficulty."

Fenwick gazed at Nancy with unbelieving eyes for a moment, then, as he saw that she meant what she said, he got out of his chair, and dropped to his knees, throwing his arms about her as he did so.

"Nancy! Oh, Nancy," he cried, in a tone of anguish, "do you mean that? Can you mean it? After what I have done can you still feel love for me?"

The girl bent down, and, taking hold of his arm, drew him up to her.

"I do mean it, Wilbur," she said quietly. "I do love you, and what I have given you is still yours; but before it shall be yours to keep for always, you shall have to prove yourself worthy of it. My life has not been happy during the past two years, and I have to work very hard, as you know. But I get sufficient to keep this little home together, and I would never give it up to marry a man who could not guard me as he should, no matter how much I might love him. You must confess, Wilbur, that it does not argue much love for me to risk our whole future as you have done over this matter. Therefore, I shall not marry you until you have redeemed yourself over this matter. But if you are man enough to do so, then I will help you to the full extent of my power."

"I will do anything—anything," he cried brokenly. "Only try me, Nancy."

"Then get up, Wilbur. I wish to speak to you," she said.

He tumbled to his feet and threw his arms about her, but she put him away gently.

"Not that—now," she said. "Sit down, Wilbur. This situation needs our coolest thought, and I must ask you some questions. It is now nine o'clock, and you say if you are not at the Hotel Venetia by half-past eleven this man Beauremon will post an anonymous letter to the bank, telling them what you have done. Do you really think he will keep his word?"

"I am sure of it, Nancy," replied Fenwick.

"In that case we must act quickly," she said. "Now, listen, Wilbur. How much did you borrow the first time when you had to pay the ten-shilling call on your shares?"

"Six hundred pounds."

"That is a large sum. Is there no way you can fix it up so it won't be discovered?"

"I could if it weren't for the letter this man Beauremon will send."

"Ah! I had forgotten about that for the moment. So the situation is simply this. If you go to the Hotel Venetia and hand over this fifty thousand pounds to Beauremon, he will take the money and decamp. Then, when the thing is discovered, he will be far away, and you will be left to face the music?"

"That is the case, Nancy."

"I cannot see what you have to gain, then, by giving him the money."

"There is just a chance, Nancy, that the bank will not discover that I did it."

"The bank will never have the opportunity to doubt," she responded quickly. "This money will never go to Beauremon, no matter what the result. It is going to stay in my possession until I decide what is the best thing to do with it. Basing our actions on that, it seems certain that to-morrow, by the first post, your bank will be informed of what you have done. Even if this fifty thousand pounds is turned to them, they will still have the six hundred against you. You might borrow the sum and pay it back; but, even so, your career with the bank is finished. You will have to make an entirely fresh start. Therefore, although I intend seeing that the bank gets every penny of this money, I shall not send it back to them until I know what is the best way to do so. As long as I hold the money I have a powerful weapon in my hands. It might serve eventually to influence them to take no measures against you. But we shall see about that. Now, what do you propose doing? Where will you go?"

The young fellow shook his head.

"I don't know, Nancy," he replied, as a look of fear came into his eyes. "I cannot go back to the bank, and I shall be a hunted man."

"That is true," she agreed. It may seem that she was cold and somewhat merciless in her treatment of Fenwick, but, on the contrary, her heart was aching with love and tenderness for him.

She realised, however, that it was a serious situation which needed all their wits to circumvent, and if she did not deal with the affair in a decisive manner, they would be lost.

She was already learning the responsibilities of life, and it was costing her dearly.

"Then if you have no plans, Wilbur, you shall have to let me think of something," she went on. "Will you leave yourself in my hands?"

"Absolutely and completely, Nancy," he replied earnestly. "Whatever you tell me to do I will do. If you tell me to go and give myself up, I will do so."

"I am not going to tell you to do that," she said. "I may be doing wrong; I may be making a mistake, but I will risk it. Get your hat and coat, Wilbur. I shall get mine also. We must go out, and there is little time to lose."

"Where are we going?" he asked, as he rose to do her bidding.

"We are not going to the Hotel Venetia," she rejoined. "That is all I can tell you now. I am simply going out to make an attempt to solve this riddle. Hurry up—there is no time to lose! I shall run in to mother and tell her I am going."

With that she opened a door which led to an adjoining room, and when she returned Fenwick was ready and waiting for her.

Before the third door, Nancy paused and knocked. She was forced to knock three times before she received any answer. Then they heard a window go up and a voice asked them what they wanted. "We are in search of a Mr. Cowling," she replied.

THEY passed along the little hall of the flat, and, walking down three long flights of stairs, reached the street. There the girl instructed Fenwick to order a taxi, and when they had climbed in she gave an address not far away.

The cab turned the corner, and while they drove along she said:

"I am going to make a call. I am going to see a girl who works beside me in the store. She had a brother who went wrong, and the police were after him. He was got away, however, by some sort of an organisation which makes it a practice to help men who have taken the wrong turning. I am going to ask her if she knows where I can get in touch with these people. She told me a good deal about it, for she made me her confidante; but she did not tell me who they were."

The cab drew up a few minutes later before a small and rather dingy house. Nancy got out, telling Fenwick to wait, and, running up the steps, rang the bell.

Fenwick saw her disappear inside, and was left with his own thoughts for a good ten minutes before she reappeared. When she reached the car he heard her give the driver a direction; then she climbed in, and they drove off.

"Where are we going now?" he asked.

"To Soho," she replied briefly. "Now please, dear, ask me no more questions. I want to think."

They were silent all the way through to Piccadilly, and on to Soho. Reaching that district by way of Shaftesbury Avenue and Greek Street, the driver turned into Hull Street, and drew into the kerb.

"We get out here," said Nancy laconically.

Fenwick got out and assisted her to alight; then, while she waited, he paid off the cab. She took his arm, and, walking up Hull Street a little way, paused before the mouth of an alley.

"This must be it," she muttered, gazing about her. "The first alley on the right, then straight through, cross the next street and continue up the alley there until the third door on the left is reached. We shall try it!"

They went on up the alley until they came to the next street, which ran parallel to Hull Street. Before the third door on the left the girl came to a stop, and knocked.

She was forced to knock three times before there was any

response, and it came not from behind the door on which she was knocking, but from the house adjoining.

They heard a window go up, and the next moment a voice asked who was there.

Nancy stepped back a pace or two and, looking up, said: "I am in search of a Mr. Cowling. I was given to understand that I might find him here!"

"What do you want of him?" asked the voice.

"I want his help most desperately," replied Nancy. "Can you tell me where I can find him?"

"Wait there!" came the reply, and they stood in the alley until the door of the adjoining house was opened.

Then they approached closer, and saw the figure of a man standing there. He signed for them to follow him, and, leading the way up a flight of uncarpeted stairs, opened a door on the floor above.

The comfort of the small sitting-room into which he ushered them was something of a shock after the dingy alley in which they had been standing. It was surprising to find a room full of books and pictures, the room of an educated and apparently affluent man, in such a place.

They could see now that the man who had conducted them up the stairs was a man of medium height, with hair slightly greying on the temples. He had a strong face and deep-set, keen eyes, which searched them both with care before he invited them to be seated.

"You ask for Mr. Cowling," he said at length, "and you say you are in desperate need of his help. How did you know he might be able to help you, and how did you know how to come to this alley?"

Nancy took up the burden of the reply.

"Mr. Cowling helped a man a little time ago, whose sister gave me the address in this alley," she said. "The name was Campbell. She told me tonight that I might find Mr. Cowling here."

"And if you should see him what would you ask him?" persisted the man.

"I would ask him to help my companion," replied Nancy promptly. "He is in trouble, and wishes to get out of London at once."

The man gazed deeply into her eyes for a few moments, then gravely scrutinised Fenwick.

"Has it occurred to you that it might be necessary for this man Cowling to be cautious. If you are seeking his assistance in order to circumvent the law, you must realise that it is dangerous for him. How would he know that you were not police spies trying to lay a trap for him?"

Nancy looked him straight in the face.

"Because we are honestly in trouble," she responded, "and because we really are not police spies."

The man walked over to the door and turned the key, then he returned and sat down in a comfortable desk-chair.

"I believe you are sincere," he said. "I am Cowling. What is your trouble?"

Nancy turned to Fenwick.

"Wilbur," she said, "tell Mr. Cowling what it is. Tell him everything!"

Obediently Fenwick began, and told briefly but thoroughly all that had happened at the bank.

Cowling listened patiently to all that the young man had to say. When he was finished he spoke.

"Are you sincere in your wish to make a fresh start?" he asked, giving Fenwick a penetrating glance as he spoke.

"I have been a fool—a crook if you will," burst out Fenwick, "but I am sincere in my wish to make a fresh start, Mr. Cowling. I am not worthy of Miss Fordyce, but she has stuck loyally to me, and says if I redeem myself that I may still hope. For that reason, Mr. Cowling, I am ready to do anything—go anywhere—endure any hardship in order to prove my words. When I am purged of this madness, then she says I may claim her. I do not know you—I do not know why she has brought me here, but I am prepared to take it all on trust. If she advises me to take the step, then it must be all right to take it."

"And this money which you—er—appropriated," continued Cowling, with his imperturbable manner. "Where is it?"

"Miss Fordyce has it," responded Fenwick.

"Are you fully prepared to give it up? It would be an essential condition of my consent to help you that the money should be returned to the bank."

"I never want to see the stuff again as long as I live," cried Fenwick, with passion. "Nancy—Miss Fordyce, has it, and she will give it to you. Send it back to the bank. It is theirs. But if you are to help me, Mr. Cowling, you will have to help me quickly, for this man of whom I told you is writing to the bank to-night. It is now eleven o'clock. If I am not at the Hotel Venetia by half-past eleven, then he will post the letter, and in the morning the bank will know everything."

"If I conclude to help you, it will be promptly enough to upset any action of this man. Miss Fordyce, is it correct that you are prepared to hand me over the money?"

For answer, the girl drew the pile of notes from her bosom and laid them on the desk.

"There it is, Mr. Cowling," she said quietly. "Please send it back to the bank."

Cowling ran through the notes quickly, and when he had verified the sum, he opened a drawer of the desk, and placed them in it. Closing it, and locking it, he turned back to the young couple before him.

"Then you are prepared to do anything to make good your words," he said, addressing Fenwick.

"Are you prepared to leave England—to leave it for a long time—to go to a far distant country, and to remain there? Remember, it will be an entirely new life. You will not be able to communicate with London. You will be forced to obey the laws of this new place to which you go. You will, if you go, be given all the opportunity you require to make good and to redeem the past, but if you disobey the laws of the place but once you will be sent from it and left here in London on the scene of your mistake. On the other hand, if you do well you will be advanced rapidly. Another thing, you will not be told where this place is. On your way there pains will be taken to baffle you. For obvious reasons, the location of the colony must be kept a strict secret. That is roughly the conditions you would have to adhere to. Are you prepared to agree to them?"

"But—but Nancy—Miss Fordyce!" exclaimed Fenwick. "How about her?"

Cowling smiled; and when he did so his face lit up in a wonderful manner.

"Miss Fordyce," he said softly. "Ah, yes; I was forgetting about her! What would you have to say to those conditions, Miss Fordyce?"

"I am ready to agree to anything which will help Wilbur to redeem this mistake," she said, in quivering tones. "But— but I do not want to give him up for good."

"Nor will it be necessary," responded Cowling. "If he makes

good, then at the end of twelve months he can get in touch with you, and if you wish, you may come to him and marry him."

"Then, Mr. Cowling, take me and help me," said Fenwick, rising. "I leave myself entirely in your hands."

Cowling also rose and shook hands with the young man.

"I will do so," he said. "But let me tell you now that I am but the agent of the place. You owe no thanks to me. It is at the orders of my—er—employer that I assist those who need assistance. She it is who conceived it all— to her is the credit due. When you reach your destination you will know whom it is that you have to thank. Now go home both of you. Hold yourselves in readiness to come with me early in the morning. Be at the mouth of the alley which leads off Hull Street to-morrow morning at nine o'clock sharp. There is a steamer leaving Liverpool tomorrow afternoon. It just happens that I myself am leaving England to report to my employer, and will accompany you all the way to the place where you are going. We will motor through to Liverpool, and Miss Fordyce can come with us, returning by train. The expense of the matter you will please leave to me. We will adjust that later on when you are well under way with your new life. Does that suit you?"

Fenwick nodded, and Nancy Fordyce, with tears in her eyes, went across to Cowling, and took his hand in hers.

"Mr. Cowling," she said chokingly, "I cannot tell you what you have done for me to-night. I know of no way in which I can repay you, but you will always have the gratitude of a very unhappy girl!"

Cowling laid his hand over hers.

"Let us trust that the future will hold more happiness for you," he said gently. "If this young man has it in him he can yet redeem himself and repay you for what you have done for him. In that I and my employers get the results which we seek. Now you had better be getting along. Don't forget to be sharp on time in the morning. By the way, Miss Fordyce, are you employed?"

"Yes, Mr. Cowling. I work at —'s, in Oxford Street."

Cowling nodded.

"Ah! Yes, I know the firm well. In fact, the managing-director of that firm is very well known to me. You need not worry about getting away to-morrow. I shall communicate with him, and you will find that everything will be all right."

Nancy tried to thank him again, but he would have none of it. He gently led them to the door, and then, with a parting caution to them, conducted them down the bare staircase to the alley.

He watched them until they had disappeared from view, then closed the door and ascended to the floor above.

Nor did Nancy Fordyce and Wilbur Fenwick as they walked down Hull Street dream for a single instant that they had been carefully shadowed all the way from Earl's Court, and that, crouching in the shadow, had been a man listening to their words even as Cowling first opened his door to them that evening.

They went on their way, unaware of this, and up in his comfortable room Cowling, too, was ignorant, of it.

He had been sitting there for a matter of fifteen minutes or so, when he heard a knock below, and, turning off the light of the room, walked to the window and drew aside the curtain which covered it.

He was going away in the morning to travel to Yvonne's island of mystery, and had had a good many callers all day. There would be several along yet, he reckoned, and, in tact, thought this must be one of those whom he expected.

Softly lifting the sash, he looked down and saw two shadows forms in the alley beneath.

"Who is it?" he asked.

"We are seeking for Mr. Cowling," replied one of the men. "We were directed here to him. Can you tell us if we are right?"

"And why do you seek Mr. Cowling?" asked Cowling curtly.

"We seek his assistance," came back the reply at once.

"Wait there," rejoined Cowling.

Closing the window, he turned back into the room and switched on the lights again. Then, pausing by the desk for a moment, he turned another switch which was concealed beneath the desk top, although what effect the turning had was not apparent.

That done, he opened the door of the room and went down the stairs. Opening the door, he peered out at the two men who stood in the alley.

"You come to seek Mr. Cowling?" he said. "Come in!"

They entered the house and waited until he had locked the door after him, then they followed him upstairs.

Cowling conducted them into the sitting-room, and, sitting before the desk, facing his visitors, gravely scrutinised them.

One, he noticed, was a big man; fair, with blue eyes, and a clean-shaven countenance. Rather a handsome man he was, taken all in all.

The other man was slim and dark and foreign-looking, but, had on his face the stamp of breeding.

That his two visitors were gentlemen was plainly apparent to Cowling.

He smiled urbanely, and addressed the fair man:

"I am Mr. Cowling," he said. "Will you kindly inform me as to the purpose of this visit?"

"Certainly, sir," drawled the fair man. "Permit me to introduce myself and my friend. I am Baron Robert de Beauremon, of Paris and elsewhere. My friend is Duke Paul Servitch, late of Petrograd and New York."

Cowling bowed slightly, though, truth to tell, his pulses had leaped as Beauremon introduced himself. It was the same name which Fenwick had mentioned. Was it the same man?

"I am pleased to know you, gentlemen," he said coolly. "And now, perhaps, you will tell me why you have called?"

Beauremon drew out his cigarette-case and lazily lit a cigarette.

"I will tell you, Mr. Cowling," he said between puffs. "You had two other visitors this evening. One of them— the young man— rejoices in the name of Fenwick, and until this afternoon was the foreign exchange clerk at the banking firm of Prout, Green, & Co., whom you probably know. In the ordinary way this young man should have called on me at the Hotel Venetia this evening at half-past eleven, in order to hand over to me a packet containing fifty thousand pounds, or thereabouts. Is that not right, Paul?"

"Quite correct, my dear fellow," replied Duke Paul Servitch, with a nod.

"You see, Mr. Cowling, that he was undoubtedly expected. Well, sir, he did not turn up. I had threatened him that unless he did I would post to his firm an anonymous letter informing them of certain little— er—indiscretions of his which would get him into hot water if they knew. Still, he did not turn up, and, Mr. Cowling, the letter was duly posted.

"Your other visitor—a young lady—a Miss Nancy Fordyce, is, I am afraid, the cause of this young man not turning up. I do not know what your experience has been, Mr. Cowling, but it has been my own experience that when a woman begins to mix up in matters there is generally the very deuce to pay. At any rate, I am quite convinced that

20

this young woman queered my little game, if you will permit the vulgarity.

"You will notice, Mr. Cowling, how frank I am with you. It is because I know a little—very little, to be sure, but still a little—about you, Mr. Cowling. I know, for instance, that Scotland Yard would be highly pleased to know where you are to be found. But as—er—gentlemen of the same—er— profession, so to speak, I assure you I have not the slightest intention of informing them. I merely mention it to explain my frankness.

"Now, Mr. Cowling, I regret to say that I think this young man Fenwick no longer has the trifle of fifty thousand of which I spoke. I have calculated matters out, and I do not think I am very far wrong when I say that the money was left with you this very evening. That is where the woman spoilt my plans. She it was, I am sure, who was the cause of him coming to you, and since they seemed in a far happier mood as they went down the alley than when they came up it, I have concluded that you consented to help them. Therefore, Mr. Cowling, my friend Duke Paul Servitch and myself decided to call upon you and explain matters to you. I feel sure now that you understand the situation you will hand over the money to me without delay. That, Mr. Cowling, is all I have to say—for the moment."

Cowling lit a cigar and leaned back in his chair. For a cold-blooded statement of criminal intent Beauremon's words would be hard to beat.

The very daring of the cool rascal aroused Cowling's admiration; but he was a man of no mean calibre himself, and felt quite capable of coping with the situation.

"I am naturally honoured at the visit of two such distinguished individuals," he said coolly. "Also, I must thank you for your frankness. The purpose of your visit has been most lucidly explained. Let us assume, for the sake of argument, that your inferences are correct. Let us assume that the money which you have mentioned is in my possession. Let us go a step farther. Let us assume that I refuse to hand it over to you. What then?"

Beauremon smiled, and blew a cloud of smoke towards the ceiling.

"We will assume it as you desire, Mr. Cowling. I will tell you what we would be regretfully compelled to do. We should be compelled to handle you roughly, and if you resisted too much we

21

should have to see that you were put beyond mischief."

"Again I have to thank you for your frankness, sir." remarked Cowling. "I shall match it, gentlemen. The money was handed over to me, and is in my possession at this very moment. Would you like me to go still further and tell you exactly where it is?"

"That would be too kind of you," murmured Beauremon, gazing at the glowing end of his cigarette.

"Then I shall do so," responded Cowling. "Gentlemen, do you see this top right-hand drawer?"

"It is perfectly visible, sir," said Beauremon, "and if you will permit me to remark upon the desk itself, I should like to say that it is a remarkable fine piece of work."

"It is—it is," rejoined Cowling. "I picked it up in Japan. Well, sir, the money is in that top right-hand drawer, and, gentlemen, the key is in my pocket. Now, shall I tell you which pocket?"

"You overwhelm us!" murmured Beauremon.

"Indeed you do!" echoed Duke Paul.

"Not at all, gentlemen—not at all!" said Cowling. "I shall make good my words. The key, gentlemen, is in my right-hand trousers-pocket. And, gentlemen, there it is going to stay."

"I think not," replied Beauremon quietly.

As he spoke he made a slight movement of his arm, and the next instant a heavy automatic was being levelled at Cowling.

How the baron had managed to draw so quickly Cowling could not imagine. The movement of the wrist had been too quick for him to follow.

He glanced in Duke Paul's direction, and saw that he, too, had drawn a weapon. Still, the sight of these threatening objects and the business-like eyes which glinted along the barrels of them did not seem to phase Cowling an atom.

He smiled at them as pleasantly as before.

"Very pretty toys, gentlemen!" he drawled. "But surely you are not going to use them!"

"It will be with regret if we do so," said Beauremon, in a tone which had changed considerably. "Still, Mr. Cowling, we intend having that money, so let us drop the pose and get to business. I shall count ten. If you have not produced the key and thrown it on the floor by then, I shall fire. And I mean what I say."

"I believe you do," murmured Cowling. "When do you begin to

count?"

"One," said Beauremon, in a level tone. "Two," he continued, after a second's pause. "Three," rang out deep and clear.

"Dear, dear;" murmured Cowling audibly. "I do believe he means what he says."

"Four!" came from behind the levelled weapon, "Five," followed quickly.

"It is getting quite creepy, listening to that," said Cowling, as he knocked the ash from his cigar.

"Six!" snapped Beauremon, who for once in his life was failing to match the sangfroid of his opponent.

"Six it is," murmured Cowling.

"Seven!" came the inexorable voice of Beauremon.

"That always was my lucky number," remarked Cowling.

"Eight!" sounded with a peculiar ring in it.

"Two to go," said Cowling.

"Nine!" snapped Beauremon; and then, as the echo of his voice died away, Cowling moved his right knee ever so slightly.

It came into contact with the switch under the desk, and just as Beauremon's lips were framing the number ten something happened which upset all his calculations.

There was a sudden click behind each chair, and from either side shot out steel arms which curled round, gripping the occupants of each in a mighty pressure which human strength could not avail against.

With the shock of it the two revolvers were sent crashing to the floor, and, gripped helplessly by the steel arms, Beauremon and Duke Paul glared in stupefied—and it must be confessed angry—amazement at Cowling, who still smoked urbanely.

"I am waiting for ten," he murmured, looking at Beauremon. "Why are you so slow, baron?"

Beauremon made a strong effort to recover his sangfroid, and, essaying a feeble smile, said:

"It was well done, my friend. Allow me to congratulate you. I should have known that your confidence was not assumed without good reason. You have the better of us. Release us now and permit us to go."

"Presently—presently!" replied Cowling, as he rose. "But, first, gentlemen, I must see if you have any little souvenirs worthy of my attention. As you said yourself, we are all gentlemen of the same profession, and it would indeed be neglecting an opportunity to permit you to go without the usual formalities which exist in our profession." He walked across to the two dismayed rascals, and ran a dexterous hand through their pockets.

"Ah!" he said, as he viewed the miscellany of articles which he drew forth. "Two more revolvers, and loaded, letters which I shall peruse at my leisure, a nice little roll of notes from each, silver and gold, which I will leave with you, gentlemen, as also shall I leave your cigarette-cases and matchboxes. The letters and the money will satisfy me, I think, and, of course, the revolvers. Now, then, gentlemen, when I have locked these away in my desk I shall be pleased to release you. Believe me, it has hurt me to do this. I am of a hospitable nature, as a rule, and, if you feel that I am driving you away, I shall be delighted to have you remain where you are until morning. But, of course, it is as you wish."

Beauremon was game.

"Your sentiments evoke my admiration," he sneered. "Pray do not disturb us if you feel equal to putting up with our company all night!"

"That is just what I do not feel like doing," responded Cowling, with a smile. "Unfortunately, I have other engagements to-night. Otherwise I should be only too delighted to be your host for the night. What a delightful time we should have discussing the ethics of our profession, for instance. I think we could work up a debate on 'How to Make a Haul without Working for It,' or ' If You Would Succeed in the Profession, Strike Terror to the Heart of a Youth who has made a Fool of Himself.' Of course, with you, baron, in the chair."

Beauremon made the mistake, then, of losing his temper. He knew only too well that Cowling's biting sarcasm referred to Fenwick, whom he had terrorised, but he did not lose control of himself so far as to reply.

He took refuge in silence, realising that he had bumped up against a man who was of a calibre far greater than one ordinarily meets. Cowling would have to be that to merit the utter confidence reposed in him by Yvonne.

Docking the things he had taken from them in the desk, Cowling picked up the two revolvers from the floor, and, after examining the cartridge clips, laid one on the desk.

With the other in his hand, he bent down and turned the switch under the desk. Immediately the steel arms flew back into place, and his two unwelcome visitors were free. But this time Cowling had the drop on them.

"Now, gentlemen," he said smoothly, "there is the door. Do not let me hurry you, but I should like to remind you again that I have other engagements this evening."

Beauremon and Duke Paul got to their feet. The baron was too old a hand to make a fool of himself. He had come there certain of gaining his ends, and the tables had been turned on him with a vengeance.

He knew that behind Cowling's velvet tones lay a will of steel and a nerve which would rise to any occasion. He was wise enough to realise that he was beaten, and, swallowing the chagrin he felt he coolly drew out his cigarette-case.

"I quite understand," he remarked, as he lit a fresh weed. "I shouldn't dream of trespassing under such circumstances. But I can assure you, Mr. Cowling, that Duke Paul and myself will take great pleasure in calling upon you in the near future."

"Gentlemen; you honour me," murmured Cowling. "And now, in case you may not be certain of the way, permit me to see you down the stairs. The door is there, gentlemen!"

Beauremon made a sign to Duke Paul, and after they had both bowed formally to Cowling, they made for the door. Cowling came after them with the revolver held ready in his hand, and so he watched them down the stairs to the street.

He stood in the alley until they had disappeared from view, and then, with an odd little smile playing about his lips, he re-entered the house.

"They are a delightful pair," he remarked to himself, as he ascended the stairs. "I fancy, though, I gave our clever friend a bit of a surprise. It was a situation after mademoiselle's heart. It is a pity she was not here to see it. But seriously, they are well on the trail of young Fenwick, and unless we move warily, they will yet succeed in spoiling my plans. I think—yes, I am sure, it will be the best plan to alter entirely my arrangements for to-morrow. I shall see to it at once."

With that he sat down at the desk, and, with the little clock ticking merrily as though pleased with the victory of its owner,

Cowling began to frame his plans.

Tinker paused amazed on the threshold. For in the room he saw a figure lying in a chair, bound and gagged, whilst Beauremon and Duke Paul were creeping towards him.

SEXTON BLAKE had just finished a short but exceedingly important telephone conversation with the banking firm of Prout, Green & Co., and was just hanging up the receiver when the door of the consulting-room opened.

Glancing up, Sexton Blake saw Mrs. Bardell enter with a look of strong disapproval on her homely countenance. Directly behind her came a shabby, nondescript individual, whose unshaven face and baggy, ill-assorted clothes, spoke of a life lived in the reek and smoke of the underworld.

He held a greasy hat in his hand, which he twirled nervously under the stern eye of Mrs. Bardell, but when that guardian of the Blake household had departed, with a scarcely-concealed sniff, the nondescript one grinned.

Blake recognised the fellow at once. Some little time before he had had occasion to go to a particularly unsavoury part of Soho, and by chance had made use of the local knowledge of the district possessed by a ragged and unkempt denizen whom he had found there. The man who had just come into the consulting-room was he.

On the occasion in question Blake had used the fellow generously—some would have said too generously—but during a long career spent in the labyrinth into which escaping criminals speed, Blake had more than once found his generosity repay him dividends when he least expected them.

He was to collect just such a dividend on this morning, though he didn't know it yet.

"Well, Shifty Morgan," he said, after a slow scrutiny of his weird-looking visitor, "and what brings you up to Baker Street this morning?"

"I was hoping as how you would remember me, guv'nor," replied Shifty Morgan, with another grin, half pleasure and half embarrassment.

"I ain't never forgot what you done for me, guv'nor. You treated me white, you did, and I says to you then, I says, 'If ever Shifty Morgan can turn a deal for you, he'll do it.' Guv'nor, that fiver you guv me that time fairly put me on my feet, it did."

"I am glad to hear that," said Blake, with a smile. "Sit down, Shifty, and let me hear what you have to say."

Shifty Morgan sat down gingerly on the edge of a straight chair, and, clinching his hat between his knees, prepared to deliver himself of the information which had brought him up to Baker Street.

"You remember, guv'nor, when I met you down in Hull Street Alley, and you was looking for an old cellar up the alley?"

Shifty Morgan was referring to the time when Blake first suspected the existence of an underground clearing-house for fugitives from justice, and when, with the assistance of Shifty Morgan, he had located the cellar used by Cowling, Yvonne's agent.

Blake nodded.

"I remember it very well indeed, Shifty. Is it about that you have come to see me this morning?"

"It is, guv'nor. Ever since that time I've kept a pretty close watch on that cellar, and when I wasn't round, my old woman has given a look now and then. Well, guv'nor, there has been something going on round there lately, and last night—last night, guv'nor, some things happened that I thought you might like to know. It may not interest you, guv'nor, but there it is if you want it."

"By all means tell me what you know," responded Blake. "If it should prove of any use to me, I shall, of course, pay you well for the information."

"Well, guv'nor, I'll tell you how it is," said Shifty Morgan.

"Last night I was going down the alley to Hull Street. It was pretty late, but I had a little job on that it ain't necessary to speak about. I was going down the alley, as I told you, when I see two people turn into it. If you remember, guv'nor, there be a lot of old empty cases just about opposite the cellar what you was looking at, and I just popped in behind them. I thought the couple would go through the alley, and I didn't want to be seen.

"Well, guv'nor, they stopped just in front of the cellar door, and began to bang on it. I began to get suspicious-like then, guv'nor, but I got busy in earnest when a window in the house adjoining was opened, and a man poked his head out.

"Honest to goodness, guv'nor, I didn't know anybody lived in the house next to the old cellar. He hollered down, and asked the couple what they wanted. They told him as how they was looking for a Mr. Cowling; and, remembering what had happened a little while ago, I thought the name sounded familiar-like.

"After a parley, he came down and let them in, and they was in there for a good half-hour. I was lying behind the boxes when they came out, and just as the door opened I heard a voice saying 'Liverpool to-morrow.' They had some more talk, and the couple—a young fellow and a girl, guv'nor— walked down the alley. I was just thinking of going after them, and was crawling out from behind the boxes, when I see them turn into Hull Street, and then another couple comes into the alley.

"This couple was men, and I popped behind the boxes again. Well, guv'nor, would you believe it, they stopped in front of the old cellar, and began to pound on the door. The same thing happened then that happened before. The window in the next house was opened, and a man put his head out. He asked them what they wanted, and they said they was looking for Mr. Cowling. After he had a short parley with them he came down and let them in. They was there about half an hour, too, guv'nor, then the door opened and they come out.

"But the man who had let them in was close behind them, with a revolver in his hand, and he kept it levelled at them, guv'nor, until they had left the lane. When they had gone, guv'nor, the man closed the door of the house.

"I was getting interested now, guv'nor, and stuck behind the boxes. Perhaps an hour or so later the door of the house opened again, and a man came out. He slammed the door after him, and walked down the alley to Hull Street.

"I slipped along after him, guv'nor, and followed him to a garage off Shaftesbury Avenue. He got into a car there, and drove away. I didn't know what to do then, so I went back to the alley, and will you believe it, guv'nor, I had no more than got in there before a couple of men jumped out from behind the boxes where I had been hiding and grabbed me. They held a light under my eyes, and made me tell them who I was and what I was. When they was satisfied they let me go, and told me if I was wise I would not come past again.

"From my shack up the alley I kept an eye out, and I've seen enough during the night to tell me the whole place was besieged, guv'nor. Regular ring around it, there was—about ten or a dozen men, I should say. Well, just before daylight I crawled down the alley, and, slipping into a corner I knew, I watched what was going on. I was just in time to see three of the gang go up to the house what I told you about, and after a few minutes they got the door open.

They went inside, and it was ten or fifteen minutes before they come out again. When they did they was swearing lively-like, and I heard one of them say, 'Gone! Given us the slip!'

"He whistled to the rest of the gang, and they got out of the alley as fast as they could. I started after them, guv'nor, but they got into a couple of motor-cars in Greek Street, and cleared out. I thought it over, and then my old woman and me decided I oughter come on to see you about it. It may not interest you, guv'nor, but that's wot happened, and as it is, you are welcome to it!"

Blake had listened to Shifty Morgan's tale with a good deal of silent interest. When the shabby little gutter-man had finished, Blake thrust his hand in his pocket and drew out a sovereign.

"Here you are, Shifty." he said, as he passed it over.

"Your information may or may not be of use to me. At any rate, I shall keep it in mind. It seems to touch on the man Cowling, and that, naturally, excites my interest at once. I did not think he would be bold enough to return to the alley; but in a way, I suppose, he was safer there than anywhere else. The police would scarcely think he would go back to the house adjoining the cellar he used to use. I hold no special brief to investigate what he may be doing there at present, but you had better go back to the alley, Shifty, and keep watch. Let me know if anything develops."

"I'll do it, guv'nor. You can count on me to come and report if I see anything."

Blake nodded, and, dismissing the queer, shabby little man, turned back to his desk. Pressing a button, he sat drumming with his fingers on the edge of the desk until the door leading to the side corridor, and thence to the laboratory, opened, and Tinker appeared.

"Ring up for the car, my lad." said Blake curtly. "I have an appointment in the City and wish you to go along with me."

Ten minutes later they were speeding Citywards in the big grey car, with Tinker at the wheel, and Blake sitting in front beside him. They drew up before a solid but dingy-looking building a short distance from the Bank, and, telling the lad to wait, Blake passed up the steps. It was the offices of Prout, Green & Co., the big private bankers, and Blake's visit to them was a result of his telephone conversation that morning.

On entering the main office he presented his card to a clerk, who disappeared with it behind a high oak screen, which seemed to shut off a door. He returned a few moments later to request Blake to follow him, and then Blake saw that a door did exist behind the screen.

It opened into a large, well-furnished office, and as he stepped in over the threshold he took keen note of what the room contained, from the heavy, somewhat ponderous-looking furniture to the small and elderly man, who seemed almost lost to view behind a great mahogany desk.

The clerk announced him, then withdrew, and with the closing of the door the little man rose. Blake saw then that he had to deal with a dwarf, for Prout, the senior partner of the great banking firm, was less than five feet in height. But though his body was twisted and dwarfed by malicious Fate, his head was one of the finest Blake had ever seen.

It was leonine, massive, and beautifully-shaped—the head of a thinker, the receptacle of a magnificent brain.

He shot out his hand with a queer, nervous gesture, and gripped Blake's. Then he spoke in the softest voice Blake had ever heard fall from a man's lips.

"Mr. Blake," he said, "I am glad to meet you. I have heard much of you, and it is my regret that I have not met you before. Will you be seated, please, and I will explain fully to you why I rang you up on the telephone this morning?"

Blake returned the hand grip, and sat down. Prout went straight to the point.

"Mr. Blake," he said, in the same peculiarly soft tone. "I have sent for you because one of my most trusted clerks has gone away, and with him has gone some fifty thousand pounds of this firm's money. I speak of the clerk who was in charge of the Foreign Exchange Department of this firm— one Wilbur Fenwick. He was a young man for such a responsible position, but ever since he entered the service of the firm he showed an especial aptitude for the work, and was advanced on pure merit.

"Last evening I had not the remotest notion that anything was wrong, but this morning, when I came to the office, I received this letter. Will you be so good as to read it?"

As he finished speaking the banker took up a sheet of paper from the desk and handed it across to Blake. The latter took it with a word of thanks, and, glancing at it. read what was written. It ran as follows:

"Messrs. Prout, Green & Co.

"Dear Sirs,—If you will trouble to examine the accounts of your foreign exchange clerk, Wilbur Fenwick, you will find that they are short a considerable amount. Since you are not likely to put your hands on that young man without a considerable amount of trouble, it might pay you to look into this without delay.

"ONE WHO KNOWS."

Blake read the letter twice, then let it rest on his knee.

"Written anonymously," he said quietly, as he looked up— "written anonymously, and by one who evidently did know what he claimed to know. Also I note that it has been written on the paper of the Hotel Venetia. But that really indicates little. Anyone can walk into an hotel like the Venetia and write a letter. Have you the envelope, Mr. Prout?"

The banker picked up an envelope and handed it to Blake without a word. Blake studied the postmark on it.

"Posted at the Regent Street post-office, and collected at midnight last night," he said. "I presume it was delivered here the first post this morning?"

Prout nodded as Blake handed back the letter and the envelope.

"Yes. It was then I investigated the accounts. It was correct in every detail. Not only did the foreign exchange clerk not turn up to work, but, as I have already told you, his accounts were short to a large amount—roughly, fifty thousand pounds. Now I shall explain a little more. As you perhaps know, our foreign exchange business is one of the most important branches of our banking business. We do a tremendous amount in foreign drafts, and more particularly in South American paper. Here in London we handle these drafts through all the principal banking firms, but one bank in particular with which we do a very large transfer business is the P—— Bank. On going over the books I find that fifty thousand pounds' worth of South American drafts were taken by Fenwick, the clerk, and put through the P—— Bank under his own signature. He had authority to sign for the firm under such circumstances, so no suspicion was aroused when these drafts were put through.

"He cashed those drafts, and in place of them it appears he balanced his accounts by a draft drawn through the P—— Bank for fifty thousand pounds. One thing has led to another, and I find that some few weeks ago he also cooked his accounts to the extent of six hundred pounds odd. That was, however, but a fleabite compared to this haul. Success must have emboldened him. At any rate, he has got away with it, and the P— Bank informs us that the whole amount was drawn in foreign notes, which, as you know, will be very difficult to trace. From what I can discover, the whole thing was planned beforehand, for the fifty thousand pounds draft which he put through the books here in order to cover up his accounts proves to be utterly worthless."

Blake nodded.

"That is usually done by men who study out the problem," he said. "Was the draft on a firm or an individual?"

"It was made on an individual—a Baron de Beauremon, of whom the P— Bank can tell me nothing."

"Baron de Beauremon!" exclaimed Blake, sitting up suddenly. "Can you tell me if it is Baron Robert de Beauremon?"

"I can tell you that it is," replied the banker quickly. "Do you know anything about him, Mr. Blake?"

"Do I know anything about him?" echoed Blake. "I should think I do, Mr. Prout, and if his name is on that draft, I am not at all surprised that it is worthless. Not that he hasn't plenty of money. He is a very rich man, but if he is mixed up in this thing you will find that it is his brains behind it, not those of your clerk. It is probable that the clerk has been but the tool."

"It is fortunate I sent for you," said the banker. "From your words I should judge this man Beauremon to be—er— not exactly a straight man."

"Baron Robert de Beauremon is one of the cleverest and coolest rascals in Europe," replied Blake, in a tone which no man could mistake. "I have come up against him before, and not always in London. When you first spoke to me I was under the impression that this case was merely one of an embezzlement by one of your clerks, and more a matter for the police than for me. But since you tell me Beauremon is in on it, tell me all you can, please."

"I have given you the main outlines of the case, Mr. Blake. The fifty thousand pounds draft I told you of is pronounced worthless by the P— Bank. Beyond this large amount and the smaller sum of which I spoke, the accounts are quite in order. But it all filters down to the one prime fact that our foreign exchange clerk is gone, and with him fifty thousand pounds in cash. I have naturally given particulars to the police, but I also thought it best to call you in, Mr. Blake. If you can put your hands on this young man, and, what is more important, the fifty thousand, we are prepared to pay any fee within reason. The books here will be placed at your disposal, and any questions you care to ask I shall answer to the best of my ability."

"Thank you," replied Blake. "I shall, of course, desire to examine the accounts in question a little later. Meanwhile, I should like you to answer a few questions. First, may I keep this letter and envelope?"

"Certainly!" responded the banker as he handed them back. "You may keep them as long as you wish. I anticipated that, and have had a copy made."

Blake folded up the letter, thrust it into the envelope, and placed the lot in his pocket.

"Now, Mr. Prout," he said, glancing at the little man, "will you please tell me all you can about this missing clerk? A good deal may depend on some small fact connected with his private life, you know."

"I quite understand, Mr. Blake. I shall tell you all I know. He is young—less than thirty. A year ago the sports team from the office had a group photograph taken. He is in it, and I have made arrangements for one of those photographs to be given to you. As far as I know, Fenwick led a very quiet and very respectable life. He came to us seven years ago, and I know from the inquiries I made then that he comes of good stock.

"He showed a special aptitude for the work, and as he became more and more proficient, I advanced him until he became the foreign exchange clerk. He was well paid, and had a splendid future before him. Therefore this affair is all the more inexplicable to me. If he had been dabbling on the Stock Exchange I could understand it better, but I cannot find out that he did anything of that sort. Nor can I find out that he ever gambled on horses or with cards.

"For a year or so past he has been very attentive to a certain young woman, a Miss Fordyce, whose address I shall give you. Two months ago Fenwick came and told me that he intended marrying at an early date. He asked me if I had any objections, and I told him that he could do nothing better, providing the young woman was of the right type. I am cautious what my clerks do that way, so I had a few quiet inquiries made. Miss Fordyce is a young woman of the highest character. She and her mother live in a small flat in Earl's Court, and the girl herself works at —'s, in Oxford Street. They have been in London some two years now, having come up from the country.

"There, however, they were in far different circumstances, being one of the best county families. The death of the father brought disaster to them, and they were compelled to leave the country. The girl would make an ideal wife for any young man. So I am quite certain it was no demand which she may have made upon Fenwick which caused him to make such a terrible mistake.

"Fenwick himself has had rooms in Chelsea, just off King's Road. It is a studio apartment of sorts, I think, and I understand he shared it with another young man—a painter."

Blake rapidly noted down the particulars as the banker gave them to him, noting the addresses of both Miss Fordyce and Fenwick. Then, after a few more leading questions about Fenwick, he rose.

"If you will make the necessary arrangements I should like now to look at the books," he said.

The banker pressed a button on his desk, and to the clerk who answered, he said:

"You will place the books of the Foreign Exchange Department at the disposal of this gentleman at once. Give him every assistance he may need."

Blake thanked him, and, promising to see him before he left, followed the clerk to the Foreign Exchange Department. He spent a solid half-hour there going over the books, verifying the points Mr. Prout had made, and calling in Tinker to jot them down.

In addition to the information he already possessed, Blake discovered one other thing. He discovered that the first small sum which Wilbur Fenwick had misappropriated from the funds of the firm had been a draft payable through the P— Bank, and that it was one from South America on Baron Robert de Beauremon.

There was little else that the books of the Foreign Exchange Department revealed to him. He saw, of course, the pitiful tale of Wilbur Fenwick's foolishness. But it was not in the facts alone that Sexton Blake looked to read the riddle. Rather was it in the vast realm of possible deduction opened up by those facts towards which he looked.

Already had Prout's story started a train of thought. Already was there much which he marked with a strong query. Nor would he permit himself to even make those queries a definite item in the case until he had assembled all the evidence possible.

He returned to the banker's private office after he had completed his investigations in the Foreign Exchange Department, but remained only a few minutes. From the banker he had already gathered all he well could, and, with the exception of a few unimportant questions, there was nothing more for him to speak about.

But he did not return direct to Baker Street from the banking premises of Prout, Green & Co. Instead, he drove on to the P— Bank, after having received a note of introduction to the manager from Prout.

There he was ushered into the manager's private office without any delay, and found that he had a keen and up-to-date business man to deal with.

In reply to Blake's questions he returned short but comprehensive answers, and when Blake finally climbed back into the car he knew that he had found out at the two banks all that it was possible to find out until he had given the case a proper amount of thought.

On the way to Baker Street he spoke to Tinker about the case.

"It looked at first like a simple case of embezzlement, my lad," he said. "But you must have seen yourself that there was something deeper behind it."

"I did, guv'nor," replied the lad. "I saw that when we were going over the books in the Foreign Exchange Department."

Blake nodded.

"It is true, my lad. Fenwick undoubtedly has been a fool. When we lay our hands on him we will have the man who took the fifty thousand pounds, but we will by no means have the truly guilty party. It is up to us to find that guilty party; and if Beauremon is behind the affair—which we know he is—then it will take us all our time to outwit him. Fenwick is not the type which would make a good criminal. I have found out sufficient about his past life to know that he would never of his own accord bring off such a swindle as this.

"There are one or two things revealed in the books at the bank which indicate to me that he is but the tool of Beauremon, and I am not so sure but that I haven't found an explanation for that. You know of old what Beauremon is, my lad. Well, I will tell you something. The first time Wilbur Fenwick tapped the funds of the bank he did so to the extent of about six hundred pounds. That looks to me as a spontaneous attempt to get hold of exactly that amount of money. He probably had some dire need for it.

"By chance, he did some juggling with a draft for that amount, and this same draft was sent through the P— Bank. Now, I have found out from the manager of the P— Bank that this draft for six hundred pounds was not to go through that bank at all, and, in sending it through, Fenwick made his first mistake. At the same time, the draft was paid by the man on whom it was drawn, and that man was Baron Robert de Beauremon.

"Let us suppose that Beauremon got on to the fact that the draft had come through the P— Bank when it ought not have done so, then he would know that there had been some sort of juggling with the draft, and he would also know that Fenwick must be responsible for it. Let us further suppose that he went to Fenwick about it. Don't you see how that knowledge would place Fenwick in his power?"

"I do indeed, guv'nor," said the lad. "Then you think that Fenwick was the tool of Beauremon—the tool because Beauremon had that hold over him?"

"I do, my lad. I think so very strongly. You see, Beauremon would hold a whip over his head, which to a man like Fenwick would be the worst sort of spur to do wrong. He was up till then a straight-living young man. From all accounts, he was engaged to a very nice girl, and had everything to work for. Then he made his first mistake, and we see what it has led to. He has sinned greatly, but, at the same time, I am willing to wager that he personally has benefited little from it. Yet he it was who took the money, and he must meet with his just deserts.

"I am rather curious to know what sort of a get-away he has made. I am also curious to know if the girl is aware of what has happened. In fact, we must find out how he has made his escape, for we must run him down. The chances are that he will make every effort to get out of the country. The amateur criminal always does that, and it is always possible that Beauremon would assist him to do so.

"There we see the difference between the amateur and the professional. Fenwick's first inclination would be to get abroad. He would be in terror of the law. Beauremon, on the other hand, would be more likely to stick in the country, trusting to his own wits to keep clear of the police. It is to connect up Fenwick with Beauremon that we must try. Also, we may come upon some clue through the girl—

that is, if she has not gone with him. If she should decide to stick to him, then he is almost certain to communicate with her, and in that way we may get on to his track.

"Therefore, my lad, I want you to go through to Chelsea. I have written down Fenwick's address there. Go to his room, and try to make a search of them. If you have any luck there, come on to Baker Street at once and report. If you strike nothing, then you had better go on to Earl's Court to the flat where this Miss Fordyce lives with her mother. You might be able to hit on something there. In the meantime I shall drive on to Oxford Street and interview the manager of —'s, where Miss Fordyce is employed. Since the affair at —'s, when I investigated the warehouse robberies, I imagine the manager will be only too glad to tell what he knows of this young lady. I shall let you out here, my lad, and you can taxi on to Chelsea."

They had just reached Piccadilly Circus, and, drawing into the kerb, Blake held the great car panting there while Tinker clambered out. He waved his hand to Blake, then started briskly across the Circus, while Blake again started the car, and drove off up Regent Street towards Oxford Street.

Tinker got a taxi just in front of the Regent Street entrance to the Hotel Venetia, and, telling the man to drive to King's Road, Chelsea, climbed in. Blake had given Tinker the address of Fenwick's rooms in Chelsea, and when the taxi reached the corner of Church Street and King's Road the lad knocked on the window. The cab drew into the kerb, and, getting out, he paid off the man.

Then he walked slowly down Church Street, looking languidly about him, until ahead of him on the left he saw the number he sought. It was a large house, somewhat dingy-looking, and set in some distance from the road. In days gone by it had undoubtedly been the residence of well-to-do people, but now, as the card in the front window proclaimed, it was given over to apartments.

Just outside the gate the lad paused, then, after a moment's hesitation, he opened the gate and walked up the path.

"Might as well have a go for it!" he muttered, as he rang the bell. "Maybe I can get into his rooms on some pretext or other."

In response to his ring a slatternly-looking maid opened the door and stared at him questioningly. Tinker smiled in his very best manner. He was an adept, was that young man, at handling subjects like the one before him.

"I am looking for Mr. Wilbur Fenwick," he said. "I was told he lived here. Can you tell me, please, if he is at home?"

While he spoke he thrust his hand into his pocket, took out half-a-crown, and carelessly twiddled it between his thumb and first finger. The look of sulkiness on the slattern's face disappeared, and she eyed the coin greedily. Poor little wench! She was of that class which slaves upstairs and downstairs for a meagre pittance a week, having no opportunity, or, when work was finished, no inclination, for any of the little joys of life which such a coin might buy.

There are many, many such in the great City of London, many such whose days are one endless round of grey toil, whose nights are hours of heavy unconsciousness while the body seeks surcease from the back-breaking toil of the day. Is it any wonder that they are so eager to oblige when a request for information is accompanied by what to them means several days' wages?

"Mr. Fenwick isn't in, sir," she answered. "There 'ave been two other gentlemen 'ere this morning a-looking for 'im. They are waiting upstairs now for 'im. 'Is friend Mr. Gordon is up there. If you wish to go up you may."

"Two other gentlemen!" muttered Tinker to himself. "Must be from the police, I should think. In that case, they will be here to make a search of the rooms, and I guess it's up to me to get up there and see what I can see before they sweep everything out of the way. If it is someone from the Yard whom I know, they will make no difficulty about me having a look round."

Then aloud he said:

"Thank you very much! I think I will go up and wait for a little. You said Mr. Fenwick's friend's name was—"

"Gordon, sir! 'E's a hartist gentleman."

"Ah, yes; so he is!" responded Tinker, as he slipped the coin into the girl's hand.

Clutching it tightly, she opened the door wide and ushered him into the hall.

"Right up the stairs, sir," she said, pointing upwards. "There are two flights of them. Mr. Fenwick and Mr. Gordon have the whole of the top floor. It is a studio floor, sir."

Tinker thanked her, and started up the stairs. At the first floor he paused for a moment, then continued on his way. At the top of the second flight he saw a small hall, on which three doors opened. They were closed at the moment, and, advancing to the first one, he knocked. There was no response, but while he stood there he could hear the sound of movement in the next room, and, striding across to that door, knocked again.

There was an immediate cessation of the movements as he did so, and, bending close, he could hear the sound of whispering. He knocked again, and this time, by listening closely, he could hear a stealthy footstep as it approached the door.

"That's funny!" he thought. "If any men from the Yard were here they would not make so much mystery about it, unless they thought I might be Fenwick coming in. I guess I'll take the chance and open the door."

Laying his fingers on the handle, he turned, and the next moment he was standing on the threshold gazing into the room with a look of blank astonishment on his face, for, lying bound and gagged in a deep 'Varsity chair, was a young man, while in the very act of creeping towards the door were Baron Robert de Beauremon and Duke Paul Servitch. It was a dramatic little tableau that, though it did not last long.

Tinker, expecting only to find a couple of men from Scotland Yard, was dumbfounded at coming upon Beauremon and Duke Paul. They on their part were equally astonished to see the lad standing in the doorway. As for the young man in the chair, he was glaring in impotent anger at all three.

Beauremon was the first to recover himself.

"So it is Master Tinker!" he sneered. "You and your sleuthhound master are meddling again, I see!"

"What the dickens are you doing here?" exclaimed Tinker. "By all accounts you ought to be well out of London by now."

"Oh, I ought, ought I?" responded Beauremon quickly. "What do you know about where I ought to be?"

Tinker, who had uttered the remark involuntarily, bit his lip, for he saw that he had made a mistake in letting the baron know he was suspected of having a part in the Fenwick affair.

"Oh, there are many little things which ought to keep you out of London!" he rejoined. "What are you doing here?"

Beauremon shot a quick look at Duke Paul, and then moved forward a step.

"Don't try any games on me, you young fool!" he said. "I know very well why you are here. You came to these rooms, and that is enough. That means you and your master, Blake, are on this business. Very well; you will get what all meddlers get!"

With that he sprang forward, and before the lad could quite guess his purpose Beauremon had struck. His fist caught Tinker full on the shoulder, sending him staggering back into the hall. But it did not send him down, and, recovering himself quickly, he jerked out his automatic.

"Back! Back!" he snapped. "You can't work that game on me, Beauremon! I know you and your little tricks of old. Back, I say, or I will let you have it!"

Beauremon stopped short, and the snarl passed from his face.

"So," he jeered, "we have a cocky young bantam here, have we? Well, well, young 'un, come in and let's talk it over."

"No, thank you!" responded Tinker coolly. "I don't wish to go in there with you. I'll keep the open door behind me, if you have no objection."

"Oh, not at all!" replied Beauremon lightly, as he lit a cigarette. "As a matter of fact, we have quite finished here, my young friend. If you will be good enough to stand aside, we shall leave the place to you."

"And I won't do that either!" rejoined Tinker grimly.

"I am not sure, but I guess I'd be on pretty safe ground if I held the pair of you here until I sent for the police. If I miss you on one count, there are plenty of others you could be held on. I might mention the little affair of —"

But just what affair it was Tinker was going to mention will never be known, for at that moment Duke Paul, who had been sidling along by the wall, came at the lad with a vicious dive, while Beauremon, throwing away his cigarette, sprang from the front.

Crack, crack! went the automatic, as Tinker fired low. But he had no time for a third shot. Duke Paul was on him from behind now, and Beauremon was hammering him in front. Clubbing the revolver, Tinker brought it down on Beauremon's face, but just as he struck the baron ducked, and the blow, while bruising him badly, slipped off to one side without doing any real damage.

Before Tinker could strike a second time the weapon was knocked from his hand, and the two men set about him with a determined attempt to put him hors de combat without a moment's delay.

Tinker fought hard, and though both of his assailants were bigger, the lad was strong and wiry, and as he strained away the muscles of his arms and legs stood out like whipcord beneath his tight-drawn garments.

By the very violence of the struggle they staggered into the room, striking tables and chairs on the way, and sending the furniture crashing as they struck it. Round and round the room they went, with Duke Paul striving to throttle the lad from behind, and Beauremon straining hard with the full power of his body.

It was beyond all limits of human endurance that the lad could withstand such a pressure for long, and slowly but surely he was giving way.

Once they got him past the pivotal point of his resistance he would collapse suddenly, and they both knew it.

Then the little kindness the lad had done to the slattern below paid him a sudden dividend.

The struggle had not gone on without rousing those on the lower floors, and the two shots which Tinker had fired had reverberated through the hall and down the stairs.

Now there appeared in the doorway the figure of the slattern, with a look of wild, terror on her face. She took one look at the struggling trio, then gave a shriek, and, turning, fled down the stairs, shouting "Police! Murder! Police!" at the top of her lungs.

Beauremon and Duke Paul both heard her, as did Tinker, and, realising the danger they now ran, the lad's two assailants leaped back by mutual consent. They started for the door, and, with Beauremon leading the way, dashed down the stairs at top speed.

Tinker, who had staggered into a corner gasping and choking, gathered himself together, and, jumping for his revolver, raced after them.

He reached the first floor as Beauremon and Duke Paul made the ground floor, and just as the lad started down the second flight of stairs he heard the street door slam.

But already the slattern was out on the kerb shrieking for the police, and Tinker kept on, hoping at least one of the fugitives might be nabbed. He took the second flight three at a time, and, racing towards the front door, jerked it open.

Down the path he went, and, flying through the gate, stood

gazing up and down the street. He was just in time to see the fugitives reach a big car which stood up the street about fifty yards away. They jumped in, and the next moment the car was thundering towards the Fulham Road.

Tinker uttered an exclamation of annoyance, then, catching hold of the hysterical slattern, led her forcibly into the house. Tinker turned the girl over to the angry and excited landlady, whom he put off with a few curt words, then, starting up the stairs again, he once more entered the studio apartment at the top.

His first act was to release the very angry young man who lay bound and gagged in the 'Varsity chair, and when the latter—whom the lad soon found to be Gordon the artist— had somewhat recovered himself, he turned on Tinker.

"And what might you be doing here?" he asked. "What the dickens does this all mean? First, two desperate scoundrels invade the place, and without a word of explanation, set upon me. They turn everything upside-down, then take the gag out of my mouth long enough to ask me if I know what has become of my mate Fenwick. They push the gag in again; then you turn up, and the place is wrecked in a fight. What does that mean, I ask you? You do not look like a criminal."

"I should think that you would know I am not one," responded Tinker quietly. "The very fact that they set upon me as they did should be enough to convince you of that. So they came here asking for Mr. Fenwick, did they? Now, that is queer!"

"Queer! What do you mean?" asked Gordon.

Tinker scratched his chin. He wanted all the information he could get about Fenwick, yet he did not know how much to tell this acute-looking young man who had been so roughly handled by Beauremon and Duke Paul.

"Have you seen Mr. Fenwick this morning;" he asked.

Gordon shook his head.

"No, I haven't. He didn't come home last night; but when he does I will ask him to keep his friends out of here when he is away. I'll have a word with Fenwick about this affair!"

"Then you do not know if he has gone away or not?" ventured Tinker.

"Gone away?" echoed the other. "What do you mean? Gone away! Where would he go? He is at the bank, I suppose."

"It is evident he knows nothing at all about what has happened," thought the lad. "Fenwick has not taken him into his confidence. But it is a queer thing that Beauremon and Duke Paul should be here. According to what the guv'nor said, Fenwick must be well away from London by now, and if he is the tool of Baron Robert de Beauremon, then, why are the baron and Duke Paul apparently looking for him? It is beyond me. And if they found nothing here, I guess there isn't much for me."

Aloud he said:

"Certain things have happened, Mr. Gordon, which affect Mr. Fenwick rather closely. Those same things were the cause of your unwelcome visitors this morning; and, in fact, that is why I came here, too. It is very likely that you will receive a visit from the police before the day is out; but I can tell you no more, so please do not ask me. I am sorry for being the cause of some of the trouble here this morning, and if you will send a bill of the damage to Mr. Sexton Blake, of Baker Street, I will forward you on a cheque at once."

"But you are not Sexton Blake!" exclaimed Gordon.

Tinker smiled.

"I am not," he replied. "But I am his assistant, Tinker, which is all the same."

"Then what are you doing here?" asked Gordon quickly. "What has Fenwick done—got mixed up in a mess of some sort? If you think he has done any wrong you are mistaken. He is as straight as they make 'em."

Tinker shook his head.

"Sorry, Mr. Gordon, but I can tell you nothing," he said briefly. "And now I must go. Don't forget to send on a bill of the damage."

With that he slipped out into the hall before the other could ask him any further questions, and, making his way down to the ground floor, stole out quietly to avoid the landlady.

Just as he reached the street he ran against two plain-clothes men from the Yard. They stared in amazement at Tinker as he came up with them, but the lad only grinned at them and passed on.

In King's Road he hailed a passing taxi, and, climbing in, told the man to drive to Earl's Court.

During the journey Tinker rearranged his garments somewhat, for they had been badly disarranged in the struggle he had had with Beauremon and Duke Paul. He had the taxi drawn up a little way down the street from the block of flats where Nancy Fordyce lived, and, getting out, told the man to wait.

He sauntered up the street, intending to seek admittance to the Fordyce flat and question the girl's mother, but just as he reached the entrance he drew back and feigned an interest in a block of flats across the road.

Another taxi had driven into the street, and now drew up in front of the block of flats which had been the lad's objective. The driver tooted the horn three or four times, and a few minutes later a girl came out of the building. Crossing the pavement, she paused by the driver, and Tinker heard her say:

"Euston, as quickly as possible, please!"

Then she climbed in, and the taxi drove off.

Tinker kept his position until it turned the corner, then, slipping, into the block of flats, he rang the porter's bell.

That individual appeared almost at once, and, drawing out half-a-crown, Tinker said:

"Is there a family here by the name of Fordyce—a Mrs. Fordyce and Miss Fordyce?"

The porter pocketed the coin and nodded.

"Yes, they have a flat here. Want to go up?"

"Is Miss Fordyce at home, do you know?" asked the lad.

"No, she ain't. And it's funny you didn't see her as you came in. She has just gone out."

Tinker allowed a shade of disappointment to appear on his face.

"Do you know when she will return?"

"No, sir, I don't," replied the man. "She didn't say. But she took a little bag with her, and was dressed as though for travelling, so I fancy she will not be home to-day."

"Oh, well it doesn't matter much!" responded Tinker. "I shall see her again."

"Mrs. Fordyce is upstairs, if you want to see her," said the porter.

"No; it is Miss Fordyce I wish to see," rejoined Tinker. "Perhaps I'll call again."

He walked slowly until he got out of the flats, then he quickened his pace until he reached the waiting taxi.

"Five bob over your fare if you make Euston in record time," he said, and, climbing in, slammed the door.

The taxi drove off, and certainly, from the way in which he

drove, the man was making a good try at earning the extra five shillings. They dashed recklessly through South Kensington, Kensington, and Knightsbridge, and, passing Hyde Park Corner, rattled down Piccadilly.

At Shaftesbury Avenue the man turned down, and from Tottenham Court Road picked his way through to Russell Square. It was only a short run to Euston Station; and when the taxi finally drew up before the great place Tinker jumped out and gave the driver the promised tip.

Hurrying into the station, he found that two trains were standing ready to go out, and, choosing the nearer one, hurried along the full length of it, glancing cautiously into each carriage as he passed.

There was no sign of the quarry, however, so he made his way across to the second train, which he saw was the Liverpool express. He adopted the same tactics here, and when halfway up the train he glanced into a third-class carriage and saw his quarry; he felt a thrill of satisfaction pass through him.

"Not so bad!" he muttered, as he passed on. "She is off for Liverpool, I'll wager anything. The guv'nor was right. She has stuck to Fenwick, and is probably going to meet him. It looks as though he might have gone on before, and is trying to make a get-away from there. I wonder how much time there is before the train leaves?"

He was not left long in doubt on that point, for just then he heard the slamming of doors, and the guard's voice saying:

"All clear, please!"

Tinker laid his fingers on the handle of the door nearest him and jerked it open. He scrambled in just as the train began to move, and when he turned round he saw that it was a corridor train.

"This is a bit of luck!" he muttered, as he peered along it. "I shall be able to keep her under my eye; but I shall have to send a wire to the guv'nor. He will wonder what on earth has happened to me. I can write it and throw it out at a station as we go past."

By now the train had got well under way. The station had been left behind, and they were passing through canyon after canyon of dreary-looking chimneypots.

Tinker, after a single glance out of the window, drew out a notebook and pencil. Then he set himself to compose a long code telegram to Blake.

It took him some time to write it, and when he had finished

London had been left well behind. They were in the open country, with the train thundering along on her way to the North—and, for good or bad, Tinker was on her.

He wrapped up a pound-note in the message, and, opening the window, leaned out. Watching his chance as they tore through a small station, he waved his hand to the station-master and threw the message on to the platform. He caught a fleeting glimpse of the stationmaster as he ran towards the bit of paper, then he was swept from view; and, sinking down in his seat, Tinker set himself to be comfortable for the journey.

The Fourth Chapter.   Sexton Blake in a Quandary—A Concession of Sentiment—Fact and Hypothesis—The Compass of Theory Points the Way.

SEXTON BLAKE had just finished lunch, and was sitting in the consulting-room, reading a code telegram which Mrs. Bardell had brought to him at lunch. It was from Tinker, and the sending station appeared to be a small station some thirty miles from London. Decoded, the message read as follows:

"Sexton Blake, Baker Street, London.—Followed out instructions, went to Chelsea, found rooms of man mentioned, also found Beauremon, and Duke Paul Servitch on scene. Gordon, our man's mate, had been bound and gagged. B. and D. P. had been searching apartment. Had straggle with them, and would have been done for, but slavey heard, and ran for police. B. and D. P., in a funk, made a bolt for it— ran after, but they got away in car. Went on to Earl's Court to flat, and just in time to see girl mentioned come out, drive off in taxi for Euston. Made inquiries of porter—confirmed suspicions—drove through to Euston—found girl in Liverpool train. Managed get aboard. Will follow Liverpool, also wire you from there. Wire instructions to Metropole.

"Tinker."

It had taken him only a few minutes to decode the message, and now, when he had gained the sense of it, he laid it down and lit a cigarette.

"It is just as well that he followed her to Liverpool, he muttered as the blue smoke eddied across the room, lifting and swaying softly in the still air of the place.

"It is just as well, though, to be sure, I know much more now than I did this morning. So she was still in London, and has only just gone on to Liverpool. Well, I think the lad will run Wilbur Fenwick to earth there. The girl is evidently sticking to him. And yet what a coincidence Shifty Morgan's story is, after all!

"In the alley off Hull Street last night he saw two persons who were seeking Cowling—Cowling who is Yvonne's agent in London, and who undoubtedly carries out her instructions here. He is the head and tail of the underground clearinghouse for fugitives of justice which Yvonne has created, and he showed nerve in going back to the alley off Soho. But little did I think last evening that the two persons

48

who sought Cowling in the alley might be Wilbur Fenwick and the Fordyce girl.

"Now let me just consider one or two points. Shifty Morgan comes here and tells me what he saw in the alley last night. It seems that a young fellow and a girl sought Cowling, and begged assistance. From what Shifty Morgan overheard when they departed, it would seem that Cowling did not refuse them. After that two men appeared on the scene and entered Cowling's house. Until a few minutes ago I thought it just possible they might have been men from the Yard who had got on to Cowling's tracks; but now I don't know—I don't know.

"The prime point of the case is that Fenwick seems undoubtedly to have been the instrument by which Prout, Green & Co. were defrauded of fifty thousand pounds. But was the fraud the creature of his own brain? I think not. I feel strongly that my theory on that point will prove to be the right one.

"To begin with, Fenwick undoubtedly 'borrowed' something like six hundred pounds from the firm. The fraud is clear, although at a later date he paid it back. Now, if he had taken that money as a test to see if he could successfully doctor the books he would not have paid it back. But he did return it, and nothing more occurs irregularly in his books until the colossal fraud which has just been worked.

"It is more than mere coincidence that the first six hundred was worked on a draft drawn on Baron Robert de Beauremon. That was only chance that Fenwick picked that draft, for it happened to be the amount he needed, and I know from my own examination of the books that there were no other drafts within a hundred pounds of that amount passing through the Foreign Exchange Department of Prout, Green & Co. for several days on either side of the date on which he took the six hundred.

"Very well. Supposing Beauremon got on to the fact that the thing was done irregularly, which would not be very difficult, then he would know that Fenwick had done wrong. He is quite clever enough, and quite daring enough, to see immediately how such knowledge would put that young man in his power. Then comes the big fraud, and the drafts with which it was worked are like the one for six hundred, all made out against Beauremon.

"That was risky, if you will; but, after all, it was easy enough for him to repudiate them and swear that they were forgeries. By the time there was any outcry he would naturally have counted on having

Fenwick well out of the country. Very well, let me see what would naturally follow.

"When the fraud was brought off we will suppose that Beauremon would get Fenwick away. He would be forced to hand over to Beauremon most of the proceeds of the fraud, being permitted to keep two or three thousand, I suppose. In that case, then, Beauremon would have every reason for keeping away from Fenwick and using great caution not to have himself connected with the young fellow.

"But what do we find? From what Tinker has discovered, it seems that Beauremon and Duke Paul Servitch were at Fenwick's this morning. They were there on business which they were determined to carry out, as witness their binding and gagging of the man Gordon. Also, there is the attack they made upon Tinker to take into account. What does it mean? Does it mean that Fenwick was too shrewd for them, and after he got the money decided to hang on to it and make a bolt for it? That would be the first conclusion at which one would arrive; but there is another element to consider, and that element is the girl. Further, there is the anonymous letter which was received by the banking firm.

"Who wrote that letter? It was undoubtedly sent by someone who wished to do Fenwick every harm possible. Would the girl send it? No; I do not think so. From the very fact that she has gone to Liverpool, it would seem that she is sticking to Fenwick. I found out little about her at the shop in Oxford Street, but I was able to ascertain that she had been given two days' leave, and that alone looks suspicious. Then there is the fact that she has gone to Liverpool. To return to the story Shifty Morgan tells:

"It was a young fellow and a girl who went to see Cowling last night. Cowling promised to help them, and Shifty Morgan heard 'Liverpool' mentioned. Is it possible that the couple who visited Cowling was Fenwick and the Fordyce girl, I wonder? To take the theory that Fenwick got "cold feet" and confessed all to the girl, it would depend a good deal on the character of the girl and her influence over the man what course he would then take. From all the evidence at hand it would seem that the Fordyce girl is a girl of sterling character, and, being such, she would never consent to the man she loved retaining stolen money. What would she do then? It would be to her interests to get possession of the money, and send it back to the bank; but then she would still be in terror lest the bank take proceedings just the same. Her next inclination would be to seek the advice of someone whom she could trust.

"Now, the Fordyces have only been in London a short time, and the girl would not know many persons to whom she dare go. Supposing that she had heard of Cowling in some way, then she might go to him. That would explain why they might have visited him last night. She would be almost certain to take Fenwick with her, and then, when Cowling had heard the full story, he would undoubtedly consent to help them. It is the sort of case which is the ideal one from Yvonne's point of view.

"The young fellow who had made a first wrong step, the helping hand, the straight life, and the clean future. Yes; there is no doubt but that it would appeal to Yvonne. Presuming that this might be so, there once more obtrudes the point of the letter which was received by the bank, and the presence of Beauremon and Duke Paul at Fenwick's rooms. If the young fellow placed himself in the girl's hands, he would not meet Beauremon and hand the money over to him. He would give him the slip, and Beauremon would be angry. In his rage he might send the anonymous letter to the bank, and then start out to track down Fenwick.

"Is it possible that the two men who visited Cowling after the couple had been there were Beauremon and Duke Paul? If they had been men from the Yard they would never have departed as they did, with Cowling holding a pistol levelled at them. That alone is proof sufficient that they had nothing to do with the police. Then why did they rest him? Did they get wind that Fenwick and the Fordyce girl had gone to him? Is that why they were at Fenwick's rooms this morning trying to discover some clue as to where he might have gone? It would seem a very likely theory.

"If this hypothesis should be the correct one, then it resolves itself not into a simple case of running down the embezzler, Fenwick, but of tracing down Cowling, and through him coming up against Beauremon and Duke Paul Servitch. It is a three-handed affair in that alone, and always in the background there stands the shadow of Yvonne.

"Yvonne! What can I do? What should I do? Were I to work on simple lines, I suppose I should send a wire to the Chief of the Liverpool Police, telling him what I suspect, and asking him to spread the net for Fenwick. But that would not rope in Cowling. Cowling is too shrewd to leave himself open to any such move as that; and it is a safe bet that any plans he may have made he will change at once when he knows he is being tracked. Then, again, it would not lead to Yvonne; and it might not achieve the return of the money. Beauremon, too, will still be in the game, and may even now be figuring out some plan to get possession of the money before Fenwick can give him the slip."

Blake's musings broke off there, and he sank into a reverie. Generally the subjects of his thoughts were Fenwick, Beauremon, and Cowling; but away down deep there was the insidious suggestion that behind it all stood Yvonne.

Yvonne!

How he had suffered! How he had pondered! How he had longed since she had so suddenly dropped out of his ken! To Blake it had been a crisis in his life. It would have been futile for him to have denied that! He could trace back through the past the whole growth of the feeling he had towards Yvonne.

He could vividly remember his first meeting with her in England; he could recall all the stirring events since then which had seemed to bind them closer and closer together. How short a time ago it seemed since with his own hands he had handed her the pardon of the Government! Then what a vivid contrast the second part of her career had been!

She had not been the girl with the almost fanatic desire for vengeance, but the sweet, lovable soul whose whole being had blossomed with the warmth of happiness. Deeper and deeper had the ties of friendship cut, until Blake occupied the supreme position in Yvonne's heart; and as for her—well, if Blake would have acknowledged the truth he would have revealed a throbbing something within his soul which had only been there since Yvonne had come into his life.

More than once in the past had it leaped the barriers he had set about it, and for one brief instant had surged through his being, bringing with it a realisation of what she really meant to him. Then, while they seemed nearer to each other than they had ever been, her departure had come like a bolt from the blue.

Out of the past a brother had appeared. He had been in trouble. He had needed Yvonne, and, with the great generosity of her nature, she had not withheld her help. Yet it had meant the severance of her relations with Blake. How well he remembered the chase to New York, and how he and Bob Cartier had fought in the saloon of the Fleur-de-Lys! He had not known at first that it was Yvonne's brother with whom he had fought.

He had only known that when Yvonne herself had rushed upon them like a whirlwind, pushing them back the while she argued with them. And never would Blake forget the wave of relief which even then passed over him when he knew that the man for whom she had left London, had given up all that she loved, was her brother.

He smiled crookedly as the thought occurred to him. Then he had seen her once only since then. That had been in England again, when Yvonne had come to raise more money for her colony in the Pacific. Blake had run her down on board the Fleur de Lys, and had arrived in time to save Tinker from being forcibly taken to the island colony. He had spoken plainly to Yvonne on that occasion, but she had been adamant, and, knowing her as he did, he knew that once she had put her hand to the plough she would go to the end of the furrow.

What had Blake done? He had tried to forget her—to put her from his mind. It could not be any part of his to lend his countenance to her quixotic scheme for regenerating fugitives from justice. His business was to track down the wrongdoer, and bring him to recognised justice, leaving it to the power of the justice to deal with him fairly. He could not countenance such a colony as Yvonne had started, strongly as he himself might feel that it had possibilities.

Yet to say that he had succeeded in putting her out of his life would be to say that which was not so. On the contrary, scarcely a day passed when she was not with him in his thoughts, and strenuous must the evening be when he did not picture her as he had last seen her. He wanted to see her again, and, rightly or wrongly, he was glad—riotously glad—that he had stumbled upon a case which might bring him in touch with her again.

Of course, he might send a wire to the Liverpool police which might rake in Fenwick. But there was always the possibility that the money would not be recovered, and that would mean a long chase. Should he let the case out of his hands? Should he indicate to the police where Fenwick might be found, and so go on with other matters? Or should he follow up the lines of his own theories, and run down Cowling as well?

The first would mean that he would not come into contact with Yvonne; the second would mean a possibility that such a thing might occur. Cold reasoning said that he should take the first line; warm sentiment pleaded that he take the second. Either would lead to the same goal. Would he make the concession to sentiment? Would he still keep the case within his own hands?

The fact that Tinker was already on his way to Liverpool was a strong argument that he should, and whether it were that reason or sentiment Sexton Blake decided to follow through to the end the case which he had assumed.

Once he had made his decision he acted promptly. Never had he gone about a thing with more vigour than he did the simple preparations he made to leave for Liverpool.

To pack a bag took only a few minutes. To send Mrs. Bardell for a taxi was an easy matter, and then, when the taxi arrived, Sexton Blake, with Pedro on the leash, and a maidservant carrying out his bag, left the house on his way to Euston Station.

Half an hour later he was on a fast train for Liverpool, trying to read a magazine, yet conscious all the time that with each pounding revolution of the wheels his brain was beating out the word:

Yvonne! Yvonne! Yvonne!

The Fifth Chapter. Tinker Does Some Hustling—Playing a Lone Hand—A Queer Ship's Company—Done in the Night—A Message by Wireless.

IF Tinker thought he was to have an easy job of it in Liverpool, he was mistaken. He had been sent to find out all it was possible to find out about Wilbur Fenwick, and then get track of the Fordyce girl.

The first part of his duty had ended somewhat disastrously, but he had been more fortunate in the second part, and although his decision to follow her on to Liverpool had been made in a moment, the more he thought it over the more convinced did he become that he had done the right thing.

Blake had felt certain that they would get track of their quarry through the girl if she had not deserted him, and from the appearance of things it did not seem that she had. Tinker could only think she was going to Liverpool to see Fenwick, and therefore he reasoned that Blake would endorse what he had done.

Once or twice on the way he had slipped along the corridor and taken a peep into the compartment she occupied. She was there all right each time he looked, and did not see the lad, for she was lying back with closed eyes.

Tinker noted the drawn look beneath the lowered lids and the restless movements of the hands from time to time indicative of mental suffering. Young as he was, he was no mean student of physiognomy, and in the features of the girl he saw the reflection of an upright and honest soul.

"Not the sort to desert a man!" he muttered to himself, as he made his way back to his own compartment.

At Liverpool the girl had walked along to the left luggage-office, and then had passed out to the taxi rank. She had taken a taxi there, and when it drove off Tinker was in another one close behind.

The taxi ahead drove through the busy portion of the city until it came to the water front, and then, picking its way through the stream of heavy drags which passes up and down the river front, it drove on until it came to the wharves where the main body of the shipping lay.

At the head of some docks given over to great liners the taxi bearing the girl stopped, and Tinker saw her descend. He waited until she had paid off the driver, then he, too, descended, and, tossing his own driver some money, made off after her.

It was not difficult to keep her in sight in that crowded district, for the girl was too busy picking her way to notice that she was being shadowed. She went along for a little distance, and then as she reached the corner of a big warehouse which bore the name of a small shipping company, she was met by a man whose face and figure Tinker could not see distinctly, so great was the distance.

He closed up rapidly now, and, reaching the corner of the warehouse, turned into a great gate which opened on to the wharf proper. Some distance along it he caught sight of the girl and her escort, and, dodging along behind them, saw them cross a small gangway which led from the wharf to the deck of a moderate-sized-looking steamer.

It was dwarfed by the great liners which lay close at hand, but, reading the name on the bows and remembering the name of the shipping company which he had seen on the warehouse, Tinker knew it was one of a small line of passenger ships which ran between Liverpool and Montreal. He sauntered along the wharf until he came to a pile of cases, and, taking cover there, assumed an attitude of listless interest in the shipping for the benefit of anyone who might come along.

But he was watching the ship like a hawk, and for a solid hour he stood there, wondering what could have been the girl's object in coming there. Was Fenwick already on board? Had she come to say good-bye to him, or was she perchance going with him?

It was hard to figure what a woman might do under such circumstances. If that ship—the Mattapac—was to be the way by which Wilbur Fenwick were to escape from the justice which sought him, then if the girl were standing by him she might very conceivably go with him.

In that case it would be necessary for Tinker to act quickly. He knew that by now Blake must have his telegram, but he could not figure what his master might wish him to do.

Undoubtedly there would be a wire from Blake at the Metropole, but he had not had time to go there, and he didn't dare take the opportunity now. He knew from experience that the first tenet of a profession such as Blake's was to stick to the quarry once you had him in sight, and to be particularly sharp when the quarry was on the move.

He was still debating what to do when suddenly he saw a man

cross the gangway to the wharf and come towards him. Tinker shrank back still farther behind the cases, and watched.

As the man drew nearer he could make out his features, and then, as he turned his face in the lad's direction, Tinker saw that it was none other than Cowling, Yvonne's London agent.

A thrill went through the lad.

"Now, that is funny," he muttered, holding himself wanly so Cowling might not see him. "Cowling here and on this ship! Fenwick on the same ship! By thunder, I believe I have got it! Cowling is assisting Fenwick out of the country. From what the guv'nor said of Fenwick I can see that he would be quite eligible for Yvonne's colony. I wonder if that is really so?

"Hallo! There is the girl again. She can't be going with him, because she left her bag at the left luggage office at the station. And there is Fenwick himself. My word, the Liverpool police would give something to know where they could put their hands on him! There will be a tidy reward out for him! Scott, I'd give something to know what the guv'nor would wish me to do!"

A whistle from the ship caused Cowling to turn round. Fenwick was signalling him to stop, and a moment later he and Nancy Fordyce came down the gangway. They hurried along to Cowling, and as they reached him Tinker heard Fenwick say:

"Nancy says she will have to go now, Mr. Cowling. She wants to catch a train back to London. She doesn't want to leave her mother alone too long."

Cowling nodded.

"All right. She can come along with me. I will drop her at the station."

"And you won't be long, will you?" asked Fenwick anxiously.

Cowling shook his head.

"I'll be back inside the hour. The captain tells me we get away in two hours from now, so I sha'n't cut it too fine."

Fenwick then turned to the girl, and Tinker saw her go unashamed into his arms. He kissed her passionately and murmured something into her ear which Tinker could not hear; then he released her, and, not daring to trust himself further, turned and hurried back to the ship.

The girl's eyes were swimming with tears as she walked up the wharf with Cowling, but she resolutely kept her gaze ahead of her, and so, as she turned out of the big gate at the top, she did not see the wistful look which followed her until she had disappeared from view.

"There isn't much fun in tracking down people like that," muttered the lad, as he slipped out from behind the cases and followed Cowling and the girl.

"But business is business, and when all is said and done Fenwick has lifted fifty thousand from the bank for which he worked. He is safe enough to stay on board now, so I can follow Cowling and the girl. It seems that she is going back to London, and Cowling is apparently sailing on the Mattapao with Fenwick. I do hope I can get a chance to call at the Metropole and see what the guv'nor says to do. There should be a telegram waiting there for me. Anyway, I shall have a chance to wire him what I have discovered."

He was walking up the wharf at a brisk pace, intending to shadow Cowling and Nancy Fordyce, and so absorbed was he in his thoughts that at first he did not notice two men who had turned on to the wharf from the top.

Happening to glance up, he sighted them, and the next moment he had slipped through an open doorway into the warehouse beside which he was walking. They had not seen him yet, and, keeping well out of sight behind some bales, he watched them as they came along.

Not that there had been any definite recognition of the two by the lad, but in the cut and walk of one of them there had been something vaguely familiar, and on a case like the present Tinker's caution was always very much to the fore. It was usual that much turned on little, and he was shrewd enough to be suspicious of everyone who approached the Mattapac

And the more closely he regarded the two new-comers the more positive was he that he was not mistaken in his surmise. That they were disguised, and exceedingly well disguised, was evident, but beneath the disguise which each wore Tinker was certain he could discern the identities of Baron Robert de Beauremon and Duke Paul Servitch respectively.

He whistled softly to himself.

"Here's a go!" he muttered. "Beauremon and Duke Paul on the scene, and disguised. I wonder if they are sailing by the Mattapac?"

As though in direct answer to his question, there sounded the rattle of a small hand-truck, and down the wharf came a pile of luggage. As it approached, the two men whom Tinker had put down as Beauremon and Duke Paul turned and waited. The man wheeling the truck paused beside them for a moment, and Tinker could see the larger of the two—Beauremon—point towards the Mattapac.

The man nodded and went on with his load, while Beauremon and Duke Paul followed more slowly. As they got some distance away, Tinker slipped out from behind the bales, and, coming out on to the wharf, started up it. At the top he turned into the road and gazed in every direction for Cowling and Nancy Fordyce.

They were nowhere to be seen. He stood pondering for a moment; then, making a sudden decision, he turned and entered the office of the company which owned the Mattapac. A clerk who was engaged on some bills-of-lading looked up from his work and asked curtly what he wanted.

"The Mattapac is sailing to-day, isn't she?" asked Tinker, with a fair imitation of the other's manner.

"Yes, in a couple of hours," came the reply.

"Any berths left?" went on Tinker.

"She only carries twenty passengers altogether," came the response. "I think it is pretty well booked up. I'll have a look."

The clerk came across to the counter as he spoke, and, drawing a large plan towards him, scrutinised him. Then he looked up, taking in the detail of Tinker's garb as he did so.

"I am afraid there is nothing that will suit you," he said. "There is just one cabin left, a double one, and it is the most expensive one on the ship. There is usually plenty room on the Mattapac, but she seems to be very popular all of a sudden."

"What is the price of the double one?" asked Tinker curtly.

"Well, you know, you wouldn't be able to have it alone— that is, if another passenger came along."

"I suppose I'd be able to have it to myself if I paid extra, wouldn't I?" rejoined Tinker.

"Oh, of course! That would be different."

"Then suppose you tell me how much it is, and give up worrying yourself about what I want and what I don't want, I am the best judge of that. Come along, young fellow. My time is precious."

The clerk, who had been adopting a supercilious manner with the lad, suddenly altered his tactics and hastened to look up the price.

"It will cost you twenty-two pounds to Montreal on the basis that you have the cabin to yourself," he said, after a few moments.

"Then book it up at once," responded Tinker, as he thrust his hand into his pocket.

He tossed five banknotes on the counter and waited while the clerk made out his ticket. When it came to the name of the passenger, Tinker replied promptly:

"Joseph Packard."

When the details had been duly entered the clerk tore out the ticket and handed it across with the change. Thrusting it into his pocket, Tinker made to depart.

"Take my advice, young fellow, and don't be so free with suggestions," he said loftily, with his hand on the door. "By following that precept you will have some chance of advancing in the world."

With that parting shot, and while the clerk gaped open-mouthed at him, Tinker passed out and made his way up towards the end of the road.

He paused at a corner to look for a taxi, and was fortunate to get one returning from one of the big liners farther along, he drove through to the Metropole, where, as he expected, there was a wire from Blake.

Tearing it open eagerly, Tinker read:

"Am on my way to Liverpool. Good lad! Stick to the game. Will go straight to the Metropole on arrival. Leave any message there. Keep an eye out for Cowling. Have reason to believe he and Fenwick may be together. Say nothing to police yet.   BLAKE."

"Now, how in the name of all that's wonderful did the guv'nor know Cowling was mixed up in this affair?" muttered the lad, as he folded up the telegram and tossed it into the fire. "I can't figure out how he got on to that. He is certainly a marvel. Well, he is satisfied that I have done the right thing, so that is something, and from what he says I gather he means me to stick to them no matter where they go. I wonder what time his train will get to Liverpool? If he arrives in time, then he may decide to have them off the Mattapac before she gets away. On the other hand, if his train doesn't get into Liverpool until after the Mattapac has sailed, I don't see anything for it but for me to sail on her and leave word here what I have done. I'll look up the time of his arrival."

Calling a page, Tinker sent for an "A B G," and, hastily turning over the leaves, found that Blake could not possibly arrive in Liverpool until some little time after the Mattapac was due to sail.

"I might get her delayed in some way," he muttered; "but if I do, it will be for only a short time at most. I do wish the guv'nor could make it before then! The whole bunch is here, and it looks as if they are all getting out on the Mattapac. There will be something doing on that ship before she reaches Montreal, or I miss my guess badly.

"The first thing for me to do is to write to the guv'nor, and leave the letter here for him. He will come on here as soon as he leaves the train. Then I must hustle on to the station, and see that the Fordyce girl really gets away to London. When I have done that I shall have to get hold of some things to last me on the voyage. I can buy other things in Montreal. Then, if I can hold the Mattapac for a little, the guv'nor may be able to catch it."

Tinker hurried into the writing-room, and wrote a hurried but detailed note to Blake, which he left with the clerk to be handed to Blake as soon as he should arrive.

After that he left the Metropole, and, getting into a taxi, drove to the railway-station. He was compelled to hang about for a good twenty minutes before the London train was due to go, but when it did he saw Nancy Fordyce go with it, and when it finally drew out of the station he made his way to the taxi-rank.

He now drove to a big outfitting shop, and there purchased sufficient to last him on the journey. For clothes he purchased some of a rather loud pattern, and chose them a little on the loose side.

Passing from one department to another, he picked out a medley of articles which he needed, and then finished his purchasing by buying a big leather bag to put them in.

That done, he once more entered a taxi. It was growing dusk now, and as the cab picked its way towards the wharf where the Mattapac lay, Tinker could see the gleam of lights twinkling through the river mist like distant beacons in a dew-washed valley. The dank odour of the river met his nostrils at every turn, and from beyond the bank of mist came the shrill hoot of tugs, interspersed now and then by the deep-toned note of a liner's siren.

On a misty autumn night the banks of the Mersey where the docks lay are weird and mysterious, and fill one with that indefinable feeling of loneliness which comes with the fall of day.

Just before reaching the wharf Tinker rapped on the window of the taxi, and signalled the man to draw into the kerb. He had caught sight of a small hotel which would serve for a purpose he had in view, and, carrying his bag along with him, he had no difficulty in engaging a room for a short time.

Once there, he locked the door after him, and, opening the bag he had brought, took out a medley of articles. He knew that if Beauremon and Duke Paul Servitch were travelling by the Mattapac he would need to be on his guard against discovery every minute of his time. Nor would a mediocre disguise serve with a man as shrewd as Beauremon. Cowling, too, knew him, and if he were to accomplish anything in this peculiar three-sided game into which he had plunged, he would need to exercise his best art.

Therefore, he went about his work of disguise ruthlessly.

Firstly, he took the cork out of a big bottle of hair-dye which he had bought, and poured a goodly portion on his head. Ordinarily, Tinker's hair was a soft brown shade, which he was accustomed to brush rather high on his head. The hair-dye which he had bought was guaranteed to make it a flaming red, and when at the end of ten minutes or so he found himself staring in the mirror at what appeared to be a wild-looking, red-headed youth, he grinned with satisfaction.

"Heavens, I am no beauty!" he muttered, as he surveyed his work. "But, at any rate, it will serve the purpose. Now, if I part it in the centre and plaster it down flat, it should make an entirely different impression from the way my own hair was."

His next work was to tackle the straight and well-shaped nose which Nature had given him. It was always a sore point with Tinker when disguise made it necessary for him to tamper with that organ; but he recognised the importance of "profile" in a case like the present, and, using a method of which he was master, he soon had that straight nose an uptilted affair which went well with the hair.

It was only a touch he had given it—a touch which was part of the method Blake used, but it was sufficient to make the slight alteration, and the best of it was it would pass by daylight. At the most, one might think it had been sunburned.

A certain liquid which he poured from another bottle created a medley of brownish-red freckles all over his face, while a pair of spectacles made a difference in his facial appearance which one would scarcely have thought possible had not one seen it.

Then he discarded the garments he had been wearing, and donned the suit of rather loud pattern which he had just purchased. When his black boots had been changed for a pair of brown ones, and his black overcoat replaced by a long light travelling coat, he stood before the mirror once again.

"Scott! It isn't a bad job," he murmured, as he took in the tout ensemble. "I will defy Beauremon or Cowling, either, to see through it."

He rolled up the discarded clothes, and stuffed them into the bag. Then, carrying it, and walking with a rolling swing totally unlike his ordinary gait, he made his way from the hotel and down the wharf to the Mattapac.

As he reached the deck he could see no signs of any of those in whom he was interested; but he knew full well that not one of them would be anxious to appear too conspicuous.

A steward took him to the big double cabin which had been reserved for him, and the moment he saw it he was glad he had paid the necessary sum extra to have it to himself.

If Blake did turn up it would do admirably for the pair of them, and, if not, it would be most comfortable for him alone.

As soon as he had settled his effects he made his way back to the deck and sought the captain. That officer was not aboard yet, it appeared; but the chief officer was on the bridge, and sent word for Tinker to go up.

The chief proved to be a youngish man of the modern school of seamanship, and listened with urbane courtesy to Tinker's question as to what time the Mattapac would call.

"She was due to get away at six o'clock," he replied. "but we have just had a letter from the agents that we are to drop down the river at five-thirty. That will be in exactly twenty-eight minutes now. We are all ready to go, and I have sent word to the captain."

"Er—I suppose it is quite impossible to have the hour of sailing delayed an hour, is it?" asked Tinker. "I have a friend who is on his way from London. He cannot possibly reach the docks here before half-past six. I know that he would like to sail with us, and, as a matter of fact, I reserved a double cabin for that reason."

The chief shook his head, and smiled with polite regret.

"I am sorry, but I am afraid it is impossible," he said. "You see, we are only a small boat, and do not cater so much for passengers as we used to. This trip we seem pretty full up, but that is a rare thing. I am afraid your friend will have to sail by one of the other liners. Of course, if you have purchased a ticket for him, I think you will probably be able to get the money refunded. We have our orders to drop down the river at half-past five, and the captain will do so at that hour. It is quite hopeless to ask him to do otherwise. He is a great stickler for orders."

"I can quite understand that," responded Tinker. "I am sorry, but I suppose it can't be helped. By the way, I see you are fitted with wireless. You carry a regular operator, do you?"

"Oh, yes! You can send any message you wish."

Tinker thanked him, and went below again. He hung over the side, watching the last hurried work of the crew as they arranged everything ship-shape for the voyage.

At exactly twenty minutes past five the captain hurried on board, and went straight to the bridge. A few minutes later there was the rush of feet as the lines were cast off, and sharp on the minute the Mattapac dropped down-stream.

Smoky, misty Liverpool dropped behind them, the twinkling lights of Birkenhead grew dimmer and dimmer, and then in rounding the Point the gleam of Rock Light guided them out from the turbid and turbulent river into the deeper water of the Channel.

By half-past six they were well out, and even as they dipped into the swell of the Channel Sexton Blake leaped out of a taxi at the head of the wharf where the Mattapac had been moored, and rushed down the wharf at top speed.

Nothing met him there but the swishing and lapping sound of the black water, and, gazing far down river towards Bootle and Rock Light at the dipping lights of the shipping, he wondered which one might be the beacon of the Mattapac.

Tinker knew nothing until he felt a strong arm grasp him by the throat.

Tinker's resistance gave out at last, and he fell clean
over the side of the ship.

WHILE it would be a distinct exaggeration to say that Tinker's powers of analysis and deduction were equal to those of Blake, it may safely be asserted that he was a worthy pupil of his master. From concrete evidence which he might have at hand the lad could draw conclusions, individualising and generalising as he had been taught to do by Blake.

Of course, where there might exist but a single fragile thread of theory to go upon, his mind was not sufficiently matured or trained to develop a case along such lines, and therein he was at all times compelled to rest on Blake's conclusions.

Nevertheless, he was a hard worker, and it is because he patterned his mental processes after those of his master that he was making such a success of the profession into which a kindly Fate had thrown him.

Nor was there wanting sufficient concrete evidence on the present occasion for Tinker to be able to draw more than one deduction.

How Blake could have known that Fenwick might be with Cowling he could not guess, but Fenwick was with Cowling, and not only that, but on the same ship were Beauremon and Duke Paul Servitch.

What did it mean?

The first evening after dinner Tinker made for the deck, and, leaning over the rail, stared down at the tossing foam-tipped waves beneath. It was a tough puzzle for his young brain to tackle, but now that Blake had been left behind in England, and now that the handling of affairs had devolved on him, he was determined that he should do justice to the responsibility.

He had the hard fact that Cowling, whom he knew to be the London agent of Mademoiselle Yvonne, was on board, and with him was Wilbur Fenwick, the bank clerk, who had "lifted" something like fifty thousand pounds from the bank of which he had been foreign exchange clerk.

Blake had already expressed his suspicions that Fenwick had been but the tool of Baron Robert de Beauremon in the matter, and therein the lad found the greatest mystery of the whole affair. If

Fenwick had been associated with Beauremon in the swindle, then why wasn't he with Beauremon at present? Why was he with Cowling instead? Why were Beauremon and Duke Paul on board, disguised in a manner so thorough that even the lad's experienced eyes had found difficulty in probing beneath the surface?

It immediately occurred to Tinker that the whole quartette might be of the same party, that their non-recognition of each other was but a pose. But when he had scrutinised them carefully, though surreptitiously, he was certain in his own mind that neither Cowling nor Fenwick knew who their two travelling companions were. And he was equally as certain that so far his own disguise had not been penetrated.

So on this first evening at sea the situation was this: Cowling and Fenwick were passengers, and had made no attempt at a disguise. Beauremon and Duke Paul, both carefully disguised, were also on board, apparently in order to watch the other two. Then came Tinker, who was undetected by the other four, and who had set himself to take a strong hand in the drama which was unfolding.

From that point he sought the motive for it all. Once he could discover that, he would understand things better. What could it be?

If Beauremon had used Fenwick as a tool, then why should he be apparently shadowing him across the Atlantic? Was it possible that, after all, Fenwick had not handed over the proceeds of the swindle to Beauremon? If the baron had received them, then it was pretty safe to conclude that he would not be on board the Mattapac.

Therefore Tinker lined things out in this way. He figured that Fenwick or Cowling still had the fifty thousand which had been taken from Prout, Green & Co. He reckoned that in some way Fenwick had failed in his agreement with Beauremon. Knowing Cowling's business, it was not very difficult for him to go a step further, and look upon Fenwick as a repentant.

The memory of his parting with the Fordyce girl but endorsed that view. Then what would have become of the money? Either it had been returned to those from whom it had been taken, or Cowling must have it.

In that case, the purpose of Beauremon and Duke Paul in being on board would be to get possession of the money, and, coming to that point, Tinker knew it would be pretty safe to assume that such an attempt would be made during the voyage. Then where would he come in?

Tinker was determined to be very much on the scene, and, having already ascertained the situation of the cabins of each of the men whom he was watching, he had a certain advantage to start with.

About ten o'clock he decided to go below, but just as he reached the companionway he met the wireless operator.

"I have been searching every place for you, Mr. Packard," he said. "A wireless has just come through for you."

He handed the message across to Tinker as he spoke, and, thanking him, the lad continued his way. His own cabin was located on the port side, just abaft the main dining saloon, and, reaching it, he locked the door after him.

Then he tore open the envelope of the message, and read the message. It was, as he had expected, from Blake, and when decoded read as follows:

"Letter received; not all you say. B. and D. P. undoubtedly after money, F. was tool of B., but gave him slip. Has joined up with Cowling, and must be on way to Y.'s colony. Keep sharp watch on all four. Block any move you see developing. Am sailing on Empress boat tonight. Will reach Montreal before Mattapac. Will arrange. Get in touch with you there. Think unwise communicate too much on voyage, but if anything serious develops send wireless to Empress. We will pass you at sea to-morrow.—B."

Tinker tore the message into bits and thrust the pieces through the porthole, allowing them to blow away on the night wind.

"So much for that," he muttered. "Anyway, it proves that I did what he wished me to do. But the guv'nor is in possession of information that I should be glad to have. However, I will do as he says—I will keep my eyes open and try to block any move I see developing. Scott! What a three-handed game this is!"

The situation of the different cabins, which Tinker had ascertained earlier in the evening, was as follows: A large double-cabin, occupied by Fenwick and Cowling, was on the starboard side, in the same position regarding the dining saloon which Tinker's occupied on the port side. That occupied by Beauremon and Duke Paul was, on the other hand, very close to the one which Tinker had been given, and the lad soon discovered that by putting his own door on the hook and turning out the light he could keep a surveillance on the door of the cabin occupied by Beauremon and Duke Paul.

It was for that reason he had come down early this first evening out, for he was determined to give Beauremon no chance to make a move that he did not see. That such a move would almost certainly be made during the night seemed reasonable to suppose. To run any risks during the day would not fit in with the caution of a man like Beauremon.

Yet he had seen Cowling and Fenwick in the smoking-saloon as he came down, while both Beauremon and Duke Paul had joined a table of auction in the saloon after dinner. Whatever drama might be developing underneath, there was on the surface a smooth innocence of demeanour which was calculated to deceive almost anyone.

It was past eleven when Tinker finally decided to make the first move in the game. He had been puzzling out what would be the best thing to do, and had come to two main points.

Firstly, he had realised that if Fenwick or Cowling—which was all the same thing—had the money, then Beauremon would use his every effort to get possession of it. In fact, that would be his sole and only purpose for being on board the Mattapac. Once the money was in the possession of himself or his friend, Duke Paul, then he would certainly guard it closely until he arrived safely in Montreal. Nor would either Cowling or Fenwick dare to make an outcry.

That was where Beauremon had them on the hop, so to speak, for the money, it must be remembered, was stolen money, and Cowling and Fenwick were both fugitives from justice. Therefore, if Beauremon got possession of the money it would immediately shift the case to them, as far as the fifty thousand was concerned—in other words, it would extend the line of operations, and, like a good strategist, Tinker saw that would never do.

It would but double the labour of himself and Blake, for they would be compelled to keep Fenwick under surveillance still, owing to the fact that he himself was still wanted, and would still be wanted, by the London police.

Then what could he do to prevent such an extension of front? Why, try to get the money himself. And as that idea came to him he moved quickly.

"It might be on the person of either Cowling or Fenwick," he muttered as he sat in the dark cabin, his eyes surveying the passage outside. "On the other hand, if they do not suspect that Beauremon and Duke Paul are on board, then it might quite conceivably be in their cabin. I'll have a shot for it, anyway. If I am caught they won't dare to make a hallo. When all is said and done, I am the only one of the lot that dares to risk exposure, and while that is the case I hold the strongest card in this deal. I'll just reconnoitre up on deck a bit, and see how they are placed."

With that he left the cabin and made his way back to the deck. Cowling and Fenwick were both still in the smoking saloon playing dominoes. When he looked into the main saloon he saw that Beauremon and Duke Paul were still at their cards, and from the appearance of the table it looked to the lad as though the game would continue for some time.

Thinking he had the whole four well placed, he made his way below again, and, slipping into his cabin, removed the black patent-leather shoes he had been wearing. He replaced them by a pair of rubber-soled shoes which he had bought in Liverpool, and into his pocket thrust a little bunch of steel instruments which he reckoned might prove useful.

Then, watching carefully that he was not observed by a passing steward, he started along the corridor to the starboard side, where was located the cabin which was his objective.

He had just crossed the main gangway, and was bracing himself against the roll of the ship, when suddenly he saw the door of the very cabin for which he was bound open, and Cowling appeared. How he had managed to get down to the cabin so quickly Tinker could not imagine, but that he had done so was evident.

The lad made no attempt to retreat, but continued on his way, brushing against Cowling as he passed, and turning into a bath-room which was near at hand, he waited there until he knew Cowling must have reached the deck again, then he came out, and started once more for the cabin.

He could not possibly know that Cowling, the cautious, had come down to get the very thing he—Tinker—was after. If he had but moved an hour earlier he would have stood a good chance of finding the money he sought, but now it was safely in the breast-pocket of Cowling, that careful man having come down for it for a very particular reason.

It was his intention, now that he and Fenwick were safe away, to do the money up and address it to Prout, Green & Co., posting it when they should arrive in Montreal. He had delayed doing this in England in order that there should be no possible clue to their whereabouts; but this, of course, Tinker could not know.

So it was that while the money reposed safely in the breast-pocket of Cowling's dinner-jacket Tinker continued his way, and, finding the door of the cabin on the hook, slipped inside. Cowling had left on the light. And now, locking the door behind him in order that a steward might not disturb him, Tinker set to work.

He knew that he must work swiftly, for he could not tell at what moment Cowling or Fenwick might come down again. Beneath the lower bunk there was a small cabin-trunk, which he drew out and unlocked with the aid of one of the steel instruments which he had brought.

A full-sized photograph of Nancy Fordyce told him that it was Fenwick's trunk, and Tinker went through the contents with a thoroughness which missed nothing. Beyond a sum of something under thirty pounds there was no sign of money; and when he had tested the trunk for secret flaps or pockets, and found none, he thrust it back beneath the couch under the porthole, and, unlocking this by the same means he had employed with the other, he began to go through Cowling's belongings.

He found a fairly large sum in banknotes there—over two hundred pounds—but all in Bank of England notes, and having, he knew, no connection with the fifty thousand he was after. His examination of that trunk would have been an invaluable lesson to some of the Customs officials at the port for which they were bound; but, though he knew he had missed nothing, Tinker still failed to come upon the money.

He was just in the act of closing the trunk and thrusting it back beneath the couch again, when suddenly he paused in the act, and squatted rigid, listening. He was certain he had heard a noise in the corridor outside; and, while realising it might be but a passing steward, he knew it might just as easily be Cowling or Fenwick.

He waited while the footsteps drew nearer and nearer, and then to his strained senses they seemed to approach the door stealthily.

He watched with fascinated gaze while the handle of the door slowly and softly turned.

A soft creak came as some pressure was exerted against the door from outside, then the handle turned back into place, and he heard the sluch, sluch of feet as they went back up the passage.

"That was no steward," muttered the lad to himself, as he sat waiting to see if they would return. "A steward would never approach the door like that. Nor was it either Cowling or Fenwick. They would never creep up to the door of their own cabin in that fashion. Scott! I'll wager anything it was either Beauremon or Duke Paul. They are not losing much time, but, by thunder, if they can find any more in these trunks than I have found they are welcome to it! But things are getting a lot too risky down here to-night. I guess I had better make a getaway while I can."

He pushed Cowling's trunk back beneath the couch, and, getting to his feet, tiptoed softly towards the door. He stood by it for a few moments, listening; then, when all seemed quiet outside, he turned the key and opened the door. He peered up and down the corridor before stepping out, but when he saw no one in sight he made a break for it, and, putting the door on the hook, started along towards the main gangway. Arriving there, he did not go at once to his own cabin, but passed up the companion-way to the deck.

He was puzzled about that money. He was intrigued about the mysterious step which had approached the door of the cabin, only to go away as stealthily as it had come. He wanted to think.

So, reaching the deck, Tinker strolled along it to the after-part of the promenade. There he turned to pass the smoking saloon, and, peering in through the port, saw Cowling and Fenwick still engaged on their game of dominoes.

"It wasn't either of them, I feel certain," he muttered as he turned back to the rail. "It must have been either Beauremon or Duke Paul. They are determined to lose no opportunity of getting the money, and they will make attempt after attempt."

Leaning there gazing down at the black mystery of the tossing Atlantic, Tinker did not see the dark blur of a figure which came slowly down the deck, keeping in close to the shadow-fringed saloon until it got almost opposite the lad. Nor did he know that the same figure had dogged him all the way up from the deck below.

He had been right enough in his surmise that it was either Beauremon or Duke Paul Servitch who had crept along to Cowling's cabin while he was there. It had been Beauremon himself; but Tinker had been mistaken in thinking that he had returned to the deck. He had crouched in his own cabin, with the door on the hook, watching the corridor which led down to Cowling's cabin, and he had seen Tinker as he slipped out from the cabin.

Not that he had recognised the lad. He had not done so. He only saw a red-headed youth, who crept cautiously along, and made for the deck, and, while he was doubly intrigued at the entry of this mysterious youth into the game, Beauremon felt certain that he had been in Cowling's cabin for the very same purpose he had intended going there; and he felt, further, that within one of the lad's pockets would repose the money which had lured him on board the Mattapac.

Therefore, he had followed Tinker to deck, determined to strike, and strike hard, should opportunity offer. And now, with the deck deserted but for themselves—with the awning of the promenade deck shutting off all view from the bridge above—with the lad leaning over the rail all unsuspecting, Beauremon decided that his moment had come.

He crouched in the shadow for a little, then he started forward. Such a swishing did the water make as the Mattapac ploughed her way through it, that Tinker, wrapped in thought as he was, heard nothing nor felt nothing until suddenly from behind a great weight was launched upon him.

Caught right against the rail as he was, and further handicapped by the terrific surprise of at all, he could do nothing for a moment but struggle violently to get his arms free.

He could not see the features of his assailant, for Beauremon was behind him; but in the first instant Tinker realised that he was dealing with a powerful and desperate man.

The very daring of the attack was sufficient to tell him that, and he knew that he must put up a stiff fight if he were to slip clear of the grip which was holding him.

He struggled vainly for a few minutes while the hands of his assailant felt for his throat. Then, as one of Beauremon's hands slipped down inside his coat and felt for the breast-pocket, Tinker bent his head, and sank his teeth in the flesh of the insinuating hand.

Beauremon uttered a sharp exclamation of pain, accompanying it with a curse, and then Tinker knew with whom he had to deal. He redoubled his efforts now, for he was mystified as to the reason of Beauremon's attack upon him, and could only think that it was the baron's purpose to heave him over the side.

He could only imagine that in some way Beauremon had

discovered his identity, and was losing no time in dealing with him. Using his heels, he kicked out viciously, catching Beauremon on the shins; but painful as it must have been, it did not cause the baron to release his grip of the lad's throat.

Instead, he but increased the pressure, and with his windpipe compressed terribly Tinker caught one fleeting glimpse of the black waves beneath. He fought hard then—he strained and kicked and bit and heaved—he wrapped his legs about Beauremon's, and tried with all the strength of his body to bring his assailant to the deck.

But Beauremon stood like a rock, clutching Tinker's throat with one hand, and feeling in his pocket with the other. Tinker tried to call out, but the awful pressure on his throat forbade a sound, and, ignorant as he was of the purpose intended by Beauremon, he made one last frantic effort to free himself.

Once he got clear he knew he ran little or no danger. He could soon put a good stretch of deck between himself and Beauremon, and the baron would scarcely dare to chase him along the deck.

But Beauremon was equally determined, and the harder Tinker struggled the more did he exert his great strength. He was there to search the lad's pockets before he should have a chance to make any disposition of the money Beauremon felt certain he had taken from Cowling's cabin, and while he had such a chance he was determined to make the most of it.

In his eagerness to bring off his purpose in as little time as possible, he did not realise exactly how much pressure he was exerting, and when the lad came clear of the deck, still clinging to the rail, Beauremon still did not grasp that it was his own strength which was causing it.

Feeling himself held thus, Tinker redoubled his efforts, striving to get his throat free only long enough to shout. Beauremon, in a vicious attempt to quieten him once and for all, strained forward still more to crush Tinker down.

For a moment the lad hung suspended against the rail, then, as his resistance broke down, he slipped over the top of the rail, and before he could cry out or Beauremon could make a single move to prevent it, Tinker had gone hurtling down, down, down into the black, tossing cauldron beneath, while the Mattapac heaved on her way.

For a single terrible instant Beauremon did not take in what had happened, then, as it came to him, he staggered against the rail and shot a look about him.

"My heavens!" he gasped. "He is over! What had I better do?"

He listened to hear if there was any cry of "Man overboard!" but only the swishing sound of the water, and the steady throb of the screw fell on his ears. Then slowly and stealthily, even as he had come down the deck, Baron Robert de Beauremon crept back to the main companion-way and down to his cabin, while the Mattapac throbbed on through the night.

    •   •   •   •   •

Tinker's first impulse when he came to the surface and had blown the water from his mouth and nose was to shout. And shout he did, lifting himself as high as possible in the water, and sending out shout after shout after the retreating lights of the Mattapac.

Yet no friendly blast of the siren came to tell him that his cries had been heard, nor was there any change in the position of the lights as there would have been had any cognisance been taken of what had happened.

"It was Beauremon, I'll swear," he spluttered, as he struck out, more to keep himself afloat than with any definite idea in his mind. "But what on earth made him come for me as he did? I can't make it out. I would have been willing to wager anything that he had not seen through my disguise. Then what— Scott! Why didn't I think of that before? It must have been he who came down to Cowling's cabin while I was there, and instead of going back on deck he must have hung about watching for me to come out. When he saw me he would wonder what I had been doing there, and now I remember how persistently he tried to get at the inner pocket of my coat. That is it, for a fiver. Beauremon thinks I have the money, and, thinking that, he will believe that it has gone over the side with me. I wonder if he will make any more attempts to find out? If I know anything about him he will not rest until he has made certain.

"But what am I to do? If something doesn't turn up, it will matter little to me which way the money goes. Let me see! The Mattapac is going west. That means off to the right here, some place Ireland lies. There is nothing to the south of me but sea, and nothing behind me but England, and that is a long way. We should be only twenty miles or so off Ireland, but it is too much of a swim. It was a little after eleven when I went over the side, and that means I have the full night ahead of me. It will be a hard fight to keep afloat, and this water will chill me to the bone in another hour. But I must manage it somehow. My only hope is to keep afloat until day comes, and then see if I will be picked up. I think the best plan will be to swim in towards the Irish coast. We may have been nearer than I thought when I went over."

So it was that the plucky lad began to swim, not hurrying himself, not using an ounce of strength that he did not have to use. He was no coward, and he was not whimpering. He had got into a pretty tough position, and he would not give up and go under until he had made every effort possible.

He realised all the same, how precarious were his chances of life; but that did not deter him from striking out with an easy stroke, and head well up. Not until hope must be abandoned would he give in.

So for an hour he swam steadily, breasting the big combers, or cutting through them as they bore down upon him through the night. Then while he struggled onwards towards that part of the horizon where he thought the Irish coast should lie, he caught a glimpse of a floating palace rushing eastwards.

It rose away to his left, her line of lights growing gradually more and more distinct until he reckoned they could not be more than half a mile away. For some time now he had been swimming towards her, trying to gauge with some degree of correctness about where she would pass.

Now, as he saw that he was still a long distance away, he redoubled his efforts. Yards which seemed rods he covered, battling with the down-rushing waves, and breaking a way through them in a frenzy of desperation.

Plainer and plainer grew the lights of the big liner, then away off to the left it swept racing for England with mails and passengers. Tinker struggled with a sob of disappointment as he saw the ship sweep on, then he sank back in the water, and for a brief moment almost gave up. But the lad's fighting spirit came again to the fore, and, striking out once more, he fought on grimly, while the tossing, pitching Atlantic played with him and jeered at him.

    •   •   •   •   •

Those passengers of the big Empress boat which had left Liverpool that night before, who took the trouble to come on deck early the next morning, were greeted with a sight which those who still lay in their bunks through laziness or the pangs of mal de mer were not favoured with.

The officer on the bridge had been the first to see a small black patch on the water something like a quarter of a mile away over the starboard bow.

Puzzled as to what it might be, though in truth thinking it but a barrel, he had got his glasses out of the chart-room and focused them on the object.

Then, to his utter astonishment, he had seen it to be nothing more nor less than a human head bobbing up and down in the water as the owner swam mechanically. Gazing at him, the officer on the bridge saw that the swimmer was describing a small circle over and over again, and even as he jumped to give an order, he muttered:

"Bug house! Gone clean dippy. They always do that when they are dotty. Must have been in the water all night."

Then, with a precision which was a part of the discipline of the great ship, the speed was reduced, and while the boat drew round in a great sweeping circle, a small boat was lowered.

The second-officer took charge, and, with half a dozen lusty pairs of arms to pull, the little boat went dancing away across the grey face of the sea towards the tiny object in the distance.

One of the most interested of the spectators to lean over the rail and watch the boat's course was a tall, somewhat gaunt-looking man, who had been on deck ever since day first broke.

He had been taking a vigorous constitutional round and round the promenade-deck when the swimmer was sighted, but now he stopped and watched with keen interest while the rescuers came up with the object.

There appeared to be something of a struggle before they finally dragged him into the boat; then the bow was turned towards the ship, and even as the hooks from the davits were fastened on, the great liner was brought round and sent forward once more on her way.

Only when the passengers crowded along to the spot where the rescued one was being lifted out might one have seen a strange play of expression on the face of the man who had watched with such interest.

First, there was puzzlement, followed, by utter and profound amazement, then came consternation, and, finally, he emitted a sharp exclamation as he dashed forward and bent close over the rescued one. His keen eyes took in every detail of the hair, which was now a variegated array of colours, due to the action of the salt water on the dye which Tinker had applied.

Then as the keen eyes of Sexton Blake—for it was indeed he—took in the truth, he dropped to his knees with a hurried word of explanation to the ship's doctor. A moment later the watching passengers were treated to another sensation as the gaunt-looking man picked the rescued one up in his arms, and strode off down the deck with him, followed by the ship's doctor and the chief officer.

Then they saw no more, and only the ship's officers knew what transpired in the big cabin which Sexton Blake occupied.

For two days and two nights the exhausted and semiconscious Tinker battled with fever and delirium, then slowly his magnificent young constitution asserted itself, and on the third day he was able to speak coherently.

From this on his recovery was rapid, and by the time the Empress liner passed Anticosti and entered the mouth of the St. Lawrence, he was up and about again, feeling almost as fit as ever.

But it had been a close shave, and certainly it had been a kind Fate which had guided his strokes across the path chosen by the liner. As they steamed up the great river towards Quebec City, Tinker related to Blake all that had happened on board the Mattapac, and with the heights of the famous old citadel frowning down upon them, Blake made his plans for when they should reach Montreal.

They knew from the wireless operator that the Mattapac was still in the Gulf, and that she could not possibly make the river before that evening. They would strike Montreal a good nine hours ahead of her, and they had ascertained further that the Mattapac would not stop at Quebec for more than a few hours.

But Blake realised only too well what an opportunity that few hours would give to those on board, and, instead of going on to Montreal by the Empress, he decided that he and Tinker should leave the Empress at Quebec, and there be on the watch for the quarry when the Mattapac should arrive. Therefore, with Levis showing up hazily golden in the warmth of the morning sun, they passed over the side of the big liner, and sent their luggage on to the Chateau Frontenac.

The last hand in the game was about to be dealt, and Sexton Blake was to do the dealing.

A moment later, Blake picked the rescued one up in his arms, and strode off down the deck.

The Seventh Chapter.   Quebec—The Chateau Frontenac—A Strange Meeting— Sexton Blake Plays His Hand—The End of a Long Chase.

QUEBEC, the citadel city of Canada, is like no other city in the world. Rugged, bold, towering in triumph on the face of the giant cliffs which rampart the St. Lawrence River, it is a fitting gatepost to a new country—to a land where great spaces and lofty skies are above and about one.

From the far distant days of the "courier du bois" and the "voyageurs," from the days when Champlain and Frontenac and Jacques Cartier and De Monts landed in that country of virgin forests, and planted the first outposts of French colonies in the new world, from the days when Wolfe and Montcalm fought for supremacy on those very heights, and Wolfe, the gallant British general, went to his death, Quebec has been the place of first landing—the mighty St. Lawrence has been the path, and the dark pine-woods along its lofty banks have been the breath of Canada.

Towering high on the cliff, up where the Dufferin Terrace sweeps in all its bold grandeur, sits the Chateau Frontenac, one of the finest hotels in the world. Built by the Canadian Pacific Railway, as one of that string of magnificent hostelries which stretch across Canada from the Atlantic to the Pacific, it goes without saying that all that money could do to make it worthy of the pioneer company has been done. It forms a background to the gay crowds which throng on Dufferin Terrace; it frowns impotently down upon the great St. Lawrence, which for untold thousands of years has cut half a continent on its way to the sea.

To the Chateau Frontenac Sexton Blake and Tinker made their way, climbing in the "hack" which they had entered the steep and winding roads which lead to the citadel.

With a promptness which all but takes one's breath away at first experience, they were assigned to their rooms, and then, with the warm sun overhead, the white, fleecy snow-clouds away to the north, and the golden glow of Levis in the distance, they strolled out to the Dufferin Terrace to watch the crowds which were already gathering. What a conglomeration of people it was! English, Scotch, and Irish were there, some of them already feeling the warm glow of love to their new country, some but recently landed, and still feeling the strangeness of the tenderfoot; Americans who had rushed over from the States for a breath of the pure pine-woods, French habitant farmers from the little church-spired villages of Quebec and Gaspe, long-cassocked priests, who are ubiquitous in Quebec, dainty and well-dressed Canadian women, the wealthy and prosperous Canadian business man, the tourist, the globe-trotter, and what not. And each and all were wrapped in admiration of the beauty of the great river beneath them.

Away to the north stretched the purple and towering Laurentides. To the east was Levis, and the point which stands sentinel over the Isle of Orleans, where Wolfe and his brave band waited before beginning the great attack on the citadel. Then, far beyond, the pine and fir-clad cliffs on either side, until they stretched clear to the Saguenay which cuts from the north through purple and grey ravines, finer than anything Norway can show. To the south the misty blue of the hills which make the great watershed between Quebec and New Brunswick. To the west the river again as it reaches to Montreal.

Blake and Tinker took in the beauty of the scene in appreciative silence. From the autumn woods to the north came a soft odour of balsam, which filled one's nostrils, invigorating and appealing. Far out on the terrace they strolled, until it seemed that they were gazing straight down at the river.

Standing there, Blake turned his gaze this way and that in sheer enjoyment of it all, until—until he happened to look up the river, and then he drew in a sharp breath the while his eyes narrowed in an attempt to see more clearly.

"Come here, my lad," he said quietly to Tinker, who was wrapped in admiration of the Laurentides. "Come here, my lad I have something to show you."

Tinker stepped across to where Blake stood, and, following the direction of Blake's outstretched arm, looked and saw.

"Why—why, guv'nor," he stammered, "it is the Fleur de Lys, or I'll eat my hat!"

Blake nodded grimly.

"That is what I thought, my lad," he said. "However, we will make sure. Slip into the hotel, and get a pair of glasses."

Tinker sped away, and while he waited Blake paced up and down the terrace.

If he could believe his eyes—and Blake had a seaman's eye for

82

the lines of a ship—then he must believe that the yacht Fleur de Lys, belonging to Mademoiselle Yvonne, was moored in the St. Lawrence River. What was it doing there? Was it there to pick up Cowling when he should land in Canada, and take him to that mystery colony of Yvonne's in the South Pacific? It was the obvious, and to Blake the only reasonable explanation of the fact. In a few minutes he would be able to verify the fact, and then—

His thoughts broke off as Tinker came along with a pair of glasses, and, focussing them on the yacht far below, Sexton Blake took in the details of the vessel.

There on the white bow, in gilt letters, he read the name Fleur de Lys, and he knew that he had been right. It was Yvonne's yacht. Nor did he know that even as he gazed upon it he was being observed from a window in the hotel behind.

Slowly he lowered the glasses, handing them to Tinker to have a look. Then, when the lad had finished, Blake signed to him to follow.

They strolled back towards the hotel in silence, for Tinker saw that Blake was thinking. Then, even as they approached the entrance, they saw a "hack" drive up, and as two men clambered from it Tinker gripped Blake by the arm.

"There, there, guv'nor!" whispered the lad hoarsely. "Those two getting out of the hack! Do you see them, guv'nor?"

"Yes, my lad. What about them?"

"It is Beauremon and Duke Paul Servitch, guv'nor!"

"Thunder!" ejaculated Blake. "I believe you are right. But how can that be? They are supposed to be on board the Mattapac, and she is still well down the river. How could they have got here? The Mattapac does not stop at any place until she gets to Quebec."

"I don't know how they managed it, guv'nor," said the lad, "but that is the pair. They are disguised in the same way as they were when I was on the Mattapac."

"Surely the Mattapac couldn't have docked already?" muttered Blake. "Let us hurry into the hotel and inquire."

There was no sign of the men they had seen as they walked across the lobby of the hotel to the desk. It was evident they had already gone to their rooms. From the clerk Blake ascertained that the Mattapac had not yet been signalled, and that she was still well down the St. Lawrence. Then how could Beauremon and Duke Paul have made Quebec when the ship by which they had travelled had not yet touched at any Canadian port? It was a mystery.

The desk "register," with which all Canadian hotels are provided, was lying open on the desk, and, casually examining it, Blake read the last two entries.

"'Count de Courecey' and 'M. Lavine,' " he read.

He thrust the book back, and walked across to where Tinker waited.

"They have each registered under an alias, my lad," he said in a low tone. "Come along to the smoking-room until we talk this out. I have got the numbers of their rooms from the register."

They went into the smoking-room, and, sinking down into one of the great lounge chairs, Blake lit a cigarette, and gave himself up to thought. On the wall opposite him hung a great map of Quebec and the St. Lawrence, and while he pondered his gaze was fixed upon it. Suddenly he sat up.

"I think I have the explanation of it, Tinker," he said. "Look at the map over there. Do you remember that as we came up the river we passed Ile Verte?"

"Yes, guv'nor."

"Well, that place is also a railway station. The I.C.R., which goes down through New Brunswick, goes through there. The river is very wide at that point, but it has occurred to me, my lad, that two active men, such as we know Beauremon and Duke Paul Servitch to be, could manage to swim it. Supposing they slipped overboard in the early hours of this morning, and swam across to the shore near where Ile Verte is situated, they could easily catch the I.C.R. Maritime Express, which comes up through New Brunswick during the night. It would bring them straight on to Levis, and they could then cross from there. I think when we know the truth about the affair we shall discover that is what was done.

"But the fact remains that they are here. The fact is also evident that the Fleur de Lys is anchored out in the river, though, to be sure, we do not know whether or no Mademoiselle Yvonne is aboard.

"Now, my lad, why should Beauremon and Duke Paul use such strenuous measures as we think it possible they used to get away from the Mattapac, and reach Quebec before it docked?

"The only thing I can think of is that they must have managed on the voyage to get possession of the money we believe Cowling or Fenwick took from England. If they managed that, then it is a safe assumption that they must have the money in their possession at this very moment; and, since they will in all probability use every effort to get a train on to Montreal, and thence to the United States, we shall have to move quickly.

"As I remarked before, I have the numbers of their rooms. They adjoin each other. Let us take the bull by the horns, and go up at once."

"Right you are, guv'nor!" cried the lad, starting to his feet. "I shall be glad of action!"

"You will get it, unless I am very much mistaken," remarked Blake grimly, as he led the way to the lift.

They were shot up to the second floor; and, getting out there, Blake led the way along to the room which he had noticed was assigned to the "Comte de Courcey." He knew this must be Beauremon, and knew, furthermore, that if the two cheerful rascals were planning out the next step in their flight, they would most likely be in Beauremon's room. Pausing before the door, he knocked, and almost at once a voice cried:

"Entrez!"

Blake turned the handle, and stepped into the room; but it might have been noticed that he used his left hand. His right was thrust into the side-pocket of his coat. Standing just within the door, he smiled sardonically at the two men who were seated before a cheerful fire.

"Pardon my intrusion, gentlemen," he said suavely. "How do you do, baron? And you, Duke Paul? It is quite a surprise to see you out here. I should scarcely have recognised you!"

For once in his life Beauremon was nonplussed. Not that the sudden vision of Blake had caused him to lose the sangfroid which was nearly always his, but the sight of the lad standing in the doorway behind Blake had upset him. He had taken it for granted that Tinker had gone to his death in mid-Atlantic, for he had known later that it was Tinker. Now the lad stood before him in flesh and blood, and even the nerve of the wily crook was shaken at the sight.

Blake noticed his agitation, and remarked upon it.

"You need not be agitated, baron," he said. "It is really Tinker. I regret to say that he did not go to his death, as you must have thought. He is, as you see, alive and well, though no thanks to you that he is. Close the door, my lad!"

As Tinker obeyed, Beauremon and Duke Paul came to their feet.

"Curse you!" exclaimed the baron. "What do you want? What business have you butting in here?"

Blake smiled.

"I shall not bother you long," he replied. "I have just come to collect a little matter of fifty thousand pounds which you have possession of. You were too slick for Cowling, after all; but, to save trouble, I should advise you to hand it over without delay, baron."

Beauremon glared at Blake for a moment; then he made a quick sign to Duke Paul. Without a word of warning they both hurled themselves upon Blake and Tinker; but with a quick motion Blake had his automatic out, and levelled it at them, while Tinker was not long in following suit.

"Better stop just there," said Blake coolly, as Beauremon and Duke Paul drew up, cursing. "Not another inch. That is better. Now we can talk quite comfortably!"

Scarcely had the words left Blake's mouth when there was a sharp rat-tat at the door.

Involuntarily Blake turned his head, but the next second he realised his mistake, for Beauremon and Duke Paul sprang at once. Their sole idea was to make a dash for freedom, and they cared not what methods they employed in doing so.

Blake met the crash just as he turned back to them, but it was too late for him to use his revolver. He smashed it into Beauremon's face, and the next instant they went down together, while Tinker and Duke Paul mixed it viciously.

They were struggling, with no regard whatsoever to whomsoever might be without, when the door was burst open, and into the room came Yvonne, followed by Graves, Cowling, and Wilbur Fenwick. Yvonne and Cowling both carried automatics, and as Yvonne took in the situation she lifted her arm, and thrust the barrel of the pistol against Beauremon's neck.

"Stand back!" she said curtly. "Quick! Do you hear?"

Beauremon broke free, and staggered back, glaring at her, while Blake stood panting and gazing into her eyes.

"Many thanks," he said, after a moment. "You came in the nick of time!"

Cowling had already forced Duke Paul back from Tinker, and the two baffled crooks stood panting and glaring.

"Well, it seems that you hold the trump card for the moment," said Beauremon at last. "What is the next move?"

"Simply to oblige me with what I demanded." answered Blake promptly. "Better do so without any further trouble, baron. You must see that the game is out of your hands."

"What is it you are after?" asked Yvonne quickly.

Blake turned to her with a smile.

"Would you be very surprised if I said it was the same thing which brought you and Cowling here in such a hurry?" he asked. "He did get the money from you, didn't he, Cowling?"

Cowling stared at Blake in amazement.

"Now how did you know that?" he blurted.

Blake laughed.

"It was very easy. But I am afraid you had better give up all claims to it, Cowling," he went on. "That money is going back to England with me. And you," he said to Fenwick, as he suddenly wheeled towards that young man— "you are Wilbur Fenwick. I have orders to take you back as well."

Fenwick went a sickly green, but Blake turned again to Beauremon.

"Come baron," he said, with a ring in his tones which had not been there before. "Pass over the money. I shall give you just ten seconds in which to do so. If you have not done so by then I shall take other measures to make you do so."

"How do you know I did not take it from Cowling in order to return it to the bank?" said the baron, with sudden daring. "Fenwick used my name in his swindle, and it is up to me to return the money."

"Don't try that game with me!" said Blake harshly. "I was not born yesterday. You have a very good technical defence there, and since the money was stolen money, I presume you could make that a defence which it would be hard to shake. But I haven't the remotest intention of giving you the opportunity. I want that money, not you. Hand it over, and you go free at once. I will give you twenty-four hours to get across the line into the States. After that I shall speak to the police here, but it won't be about this matter. It will be about some little affairs which you could not cover up by such a defence. Do you understand?"

For a minute he held the baron's eyes; then, with a quick motion, Beauremon thrust his hand into his pocket and drew out an envelope, which had been sealed, but which Blake could see had been opened.

He threw it on the floor.

"There it is!" he said savagely. "Come, Paul!" He advanced towards the door as he spoke, and Blake stood aside to let him pass.

Duke Paul followed close on his heels, and the next moment the door slammed after them.

Blake stooped and picked up the envelope.

"I do not think for a minute that he would attempt to fool me," he remarked. "Ah, I thought not!" This as he drew out a thick packet of notes. "Just run through those, my lad," he said, as he tossed them across to Tinker.

Then, while Tinker obeyed, Blake glanced at the superscription which he saw on the envelope.

"Messrs. Prout, Green & Co.!" he muttered. "What does this mean?"

"It means that I wrote it," said Cowling suddenly. "You know so much, you may as well know more. May I speak, mademoiselle?" he asked, turning to Yvonne.

Yvonne shrugged.

"If you wish," she said.

Cowling looked at Blake.

"Will you listen to me?" he asked.

Blake nodded.

"Go ahead," he replied.

"I addressed that money to Prout, Green & Co.," said Cowling. "It was my intention to post it to them as soon as I landed in Canada. I should have done so in England, but I did not wish to leave a single trace. You know so much, there is no harm in saying that I was doing my best to get Fenwick away. You were right, too, in thinking that it was stolen from me on the Mattapac. They took it last night. I sent a wireless to mademoiselle telling her to be on the watch for them, and that is why she is here. Now, what are you going to do about it?"

"Take it back to England," said Blake succinctly.

"But he means about Fenwick," said Yvonne, suddenly taking a part in the conversation.

Blake turned and looked the young man up and down.

"I should like to have the advice of Miss Fordyce on that point," he said quietly.

At the mention of the girl's name Fenwick started forward, then he caught himself and bit his lip.

Yvonne laid a hand on Blake's arm.

"From my window I saw you looking at the Fleur-de-Lys, which lies anchored in the river," she said softly. "May I suggest that you and Tinker come aboard for lunch, and talk the matter over then?"

Blake looked down into her eyes, until it seemed that he would sink, sink, sink into the deep blue wells which lay hid there beneath the violet shadows. Then he straightened.

"I think that would be a good idea," he said quietly. "Tinker and I are at your disposal."

So it was that the sextette passed through the crowds on the terrace, and picked their way down to the docks. A little white boat met them and took them out to the yacht. As he went aboard Sexton Blake felt a deep sense of achievement thrill him. The chase had brought him to Yvonne.

• • • • •

Just a week later the acting partner of Messrs. Prout, Green & Co. opened a letter which had come with his morning mail, and, after gazing with some surprise at the thick bundle of banknotes which he took from it, he read the contents of the covering communication,

"Dear Sir," he read,—"Under same cover, and by registered post, I am forwarding you the full sum which was taken from the funds by the former clerk of your Foreign Exchange Department. I think you will find the amount intact. I might add that I have not apprehended Fenwick, but I am in a position to state that before I got possession of the money he had already made every arrangement for it to be returned to you. In view of this, I would suggest that you be lenient in the matter, and take no further steps to apprehend him. I may add that I know positively it would be practically a waste of time to do so. I wish to say further that for reasons which I cannot explain I do not care to accept any fee in this case. Kindly acknowledge the receipt of the money, and believe me, faithfully yours, SEXTON BLAKE.

"Well, I'm hanged!" muttered the acting partner as he laid the letter down. "If he says Fenwick can't be caught, then it's a safe bet that he can't. I never thought Sexton Blake would give up like that. I thought it was his boast that a man could not give him the slip. But Fenwick seems to have done so. Anyway, we have the money back, so I guess we will let the matter rest where it is."

As a matter of fact, he was a kind-hearted man, with no desire to hound a man about the world, though, if you speak of the infallibility of Sexton Blake, he will laugh in a knowing fashion, as though he could if he would tell you of an occasion when the great detective did fail. How little he guessed the truth!

THE END.
[35100 WORDS]

Quebec City and Château Frontenac circ. 1900. /drf

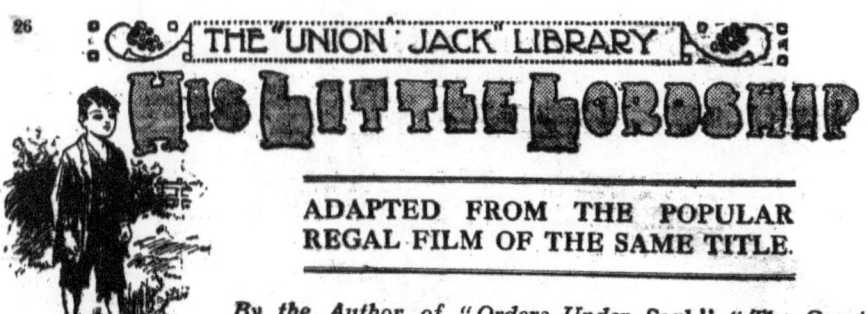

HIS LITTLE LORDSHIP

ADAPTED FROM THE POPULAR REGAL FILM OF THE SAME TITLE.

By the Author of "Orders Under Seal," "The Great Cheque Fraud," "The Mystery of the Diamond Belt," etc.

His Little Lordship

ADAPTED FROM THE POPULAR REGAL FILM OF THE SAME TITLE.

By the Author of "Orders Under Seal," "The Great Cheque Fraud," "The Mystery of the Diamond Belt," etc.

INTRODUCTION.

EZRA LING, and the gipsies of whom he is the chief, pitch their circus near the grounds of the EARL OF SHIRE. Ling and two other men, SAM FURLONG and SILAS GRIPPS, go on a poaching expedition to the earl's grounds to find food for Ling's dying child. Ling and Furlong are captured, and meanwhile Ling's child dies.

After his release from prison, Ling, in revenge, kidnaps the earl's little heir, Donald.

Four years later little Jackie, as he is now known, is still with them, but is very cruelly treated by Ling. Matt Simmonds an artiste, defends him, and in a fight knocks Ling out, afterwards leaving the circus.

In his fury at this treatment Ling smashes all the crockery in his caravan, and Mrs. Ling demands that he shall replace this by taking the equivalent to what he had destroyed from the other caravans. This he does, and then announces that he is going to try and sell little Jackie back to the Earl of Shire.

(Now read on.)

"His Little Lordship" Comes into His Own Once Again.

All unconscious of the show being enacted before them, the earl and his wife sat and talked to the little curly-headed chap, asking him many questions about himself and his life.

"Do you like being in the circus?" asked the lady.

"Jackie" shook his head slowly.

Mrs. Huntley looked surprised, and glanced at her husband.

"Why do you not like it?" asked the earl.

"They are so cruel to me," came the quiet, halting voice.

And they both noted the refined nature of the little chap's voice and manner of speaking.

"But your father—doesn't he treat you well?"

"No; I—I haven't got a father."

Again the two glanced at each other.

"Well, your mother, then?" said the earl kindly.

The boy shook his head again.

"Haven't got a mother, either," he said simply.

"Poor little boy!" said Mrs. Huntley, tenderly striking his curls. "And wouldn't you like to have a nice, kind mother and father to look after you?"

A wistful look came into the boy's eyes.

"Yes," he said slowly; "I—I should like it so much! I fell off the horse the other day, and they beat me for it! They are always beating me!"

Tears came into Mrs. Huntley's eyes.

"Poor little man!" she said. "And do you think that you would like me to be a mother to you and this gentleman to be your daddy?"

"Yes," was the simple answer.

Then "Jackie" turned his head, and started fearfully, as there came to them the voice of Ezra Ling. The next moment the latter entered with his wife.

She, with her arms akimbo, stood regarding the little scene before her with a sneer.

The earl turned, and, seeing her, rose, raising his hat as he did so.

"Good-evening, madam!" he said politely, although he was far from feeling polite.

As a matter of fact, after what the little fellow had told him, he felt more like taking the burly Ling outside and giving him a good thrashing, or get one himself in the process.

She nodded, but did not speak; so, therefore, the earl went on:

"We have been speaking to your—er—this little boy who performed so well to-night."

Again the woman nodded.

"My wife," went on the earl, "is passionately fond of children, and so, for that matter, am I, and we both would very much like to adopt him."

A sneer spread over Mrs. Ling's face.

"An' wot are we goin' ter do, pray?" she asked, jerking her thumb in the direction of the ring.

The earl smiled.

"I will make it well worth your while," he suggested.

"He's worth a lot to us," put in Ling.

"How much?" asked Mrs. Huntley.

Ling appeared to make a rough calculation.

"Well, I should think about two hundred a year," was the lying answer.

The earl put his hand to his pocket.

"If you will let us take the child away to-night I will write you a cheque for one thousand pounds, which will represent five years' profit from him. And, you must remember, in five years he will have ceased to draw on account of his age. His present attraction is his youth and extraordinary ability for one so young. In five years' time that will be different, and—"

"Yus; thet may be right," put in Ling quickly. "But, guv'nor, ye must bear in yer mind the fact thet w'en 'e's five years older 'ell 'ave increased in ability, as yer calls it. 'E'll 'ave learned himself a lot more tricks."

"Very well!" cried the earl. "I will make it two thousand pounds down, or ten years' profit! Is that good enough?"

Mrs. Huntley watched the faces of Mr. and Mrs. Ling closely and anxiously. She saw them look at each other with a question in the glances.

"Do say 'Yes'!" she cried appealingly. "He will have a good home, and—"

The woman laughed.

"We ain't worrittin' ourselves about thet; don't you be alarmed. Wot we're thinkin' of is whether it'll pay us."

Mrs. Huntley flinched at the hard way in which the other spoke, and looked down tenderly at the little, shivering youngster before her. Well she knew the kind of treatment he must receive from such a hardened pair.

"Yus, thet's it," put in Ling, taking the cue from his wife. "Wot we've got ter think about is the dibs. We—"

A hard look suddenly appeared in the earl's eyes, and he turned away abruptly. He had seen what the crafty pair were endeavouring to bring about. He realised that the boy was not so valuable to them as they were trying to make out, and that they were endeavouring to raise the sum as much as possible.

"Take or leave the offer!" he said sharply, holding up his hand, as his wife would have interrupted. "I have made my offer! It is for you to accept or reject it!"

He stooped, and, picking the child up in his arm, kissed it, motioning his wife to do the same. Then, turning towards the entrance, he said:

"You have my address; it was on the card I sent you. Let me know in the morning what you have decided. Remember, my highest price is two thousand!"

The next moment the flap of the entrance dropped, and the earl and his wife were gone, leaving Ling, his wife, and the boy standing looking at each other.

Ling was the first to make a move, and he did it with his customary thoroughness. Stepping forward, he gripped "Jackie" by the collar of his coat, and jerked him through the flap, followed by Mrs. Ling.

"Come on, yer little skunk!" cried Ling fiercely. "If ye're ter go ter-morrer, we'd better hev a little fun ter-night! It'll be our last chance!"

And I will leave it to the reader's imagination to determine exactly what form that "fun" took.

·　　·　　·　　·　　·

It was a little after ten the next morning that Ezra Ling and his wife, accompanied by "Jackie," entered the grounds of the Grange, and approached the large entrance of the house.

Ling could not help remembering the method of his last visit as a thief in the night, and he smiled grimly as he thought of the little haul he was going to make now as a result of that last visit.

The earl saw them at once in his library, and he strove to hide his excitement. He knew that the boy now practically belonged to his wife and himself, and it needed all his self-restraint to prevent him from rushing into the hall and calling for his wife.

"Good-morning!" he said, as evenly as he could, waving them to be seated. "Hallo, my little man!" he went on. "So you've come to see me, have you?"

He looked questioningly at Ling.

Ling nodded.

"Yus, sir," he said roughly. "'E's come ter stop, wi' one condition."

"And that is?" queried the earl, with raised eyebrows.

"Thet you'll swear in front o' witnesses that ye'll take no action whatever ag'in me if I tells yer somethin' after ye've landed out the brass."

The earl looked puzzled.

"That is a very extraordinary proposition," he began.

"What is, dear?"

Mrs. Huntley had entered the room, and was now fondling the boy. He told her.

"Oh, promise, dear! I must—simply must have this little chap for my very own! Promise, and get the butler and my maid in here as witnesses."

Muttering slightly, the earl did as his wife asked. It did not appeal to him at all, this business of binding himself to inaction. Besides, why should it be after the money had been paid?

While he was waiting for the servants to make their appearance, he made out the cheque for two thousand pounds, and when Ling told him his name he wrinkled his brow in thought.

Surely he had heard that name before—some place? But he could not locate where, although in the back of his brain he was perfectly sure that—

His thoughts were broken off abruptly by the entrance of the butler and the maid. He soon told them what had happened, and of the promise he was to make in front of them.

"Now, then," he concluded, as he handed the cheque to Ling, "I give you this cheque with the bounden promise that I will not take any action at all in consequence of what you are about to tell me."

Ling grinned as he took the cheque and examined it. Then he moved to the door, preceded by his wife. All eyes were on them.

"Come, man!" cried the earl testily. "Tell me what you have to say, and then be off!"

"Right you are, guv'nor!" cried Ling, opening the door. "It ain't

96

much, and it won't take long. All I wanted ter tell yer was thet ye've jest bought back yer own son!"

The earl leaped to his feet, and Mrs. Huntley gave a little scream.

"My—my—my own son!" cried the earl. "How—how can that be?"

Ling grinned more than ever as he made the reply.

"This way, guv'nor! 'E's your son, 'cause I pinched 'im from 'is bed-room one night and took 'im away from 'ere ! Thet's how 'e's your son! Good-day!"

The door shut, and there came to those in the room the footsteps of the two as they made for the hall door.

The earl staggered forward, his hand to his forehead.

"Stop that man!" he cried hoarsely to the butler. "Stop him before—"

"Your promise, sir," reminded the butler softly.

The other sank back into his seat.

"You are right. Very well," he added, as he turned to see his wife smothering the little chap with kisses; "you may both go."

He waited until the door had closed; then rose, and went to them both.

"Oh, husband mine," sobbed his wife, "he—he is really our own—our own son—our own flesh and blood!"

He nodded.

"Yes," he said soberly, taking one of her hands and one of the boy's—"yes, he is indeed our own son! Thank Heaven, we have at last found him and he is restored to us!"

He bent and kissed them both.

"And he will for ever be 'Our Little Lordship'!" cried Mrs. Huntley fondly, thrusting the boy from her and gazing lovingly at him.

"I think the better name would be 'His Little Lordship,' " said the earl softly.

"You are right, dear," she replied. " 'His Little Lordship' it shall be!"

And as the Earl of Shire turned away from his wife, who had suddenly been made so happy, he forgave Ezra Ling for the pain he had caused them both in the past.

The past had been dark and gloomy, but the present and the future held nothing but happiness and joy.

"His Little Lordship" had been lost, but was found!

The End.

Fill up the Form below and let a Hero have the Benefit of this Issue as well as YOU.

FOLD THE BOOK OVER AT DOTTED—

To...

(Or, if missing, Company Commander.)

Company...

Regiment...

British Expeditionary Force.

½D. STAMP

WITH BEST WISHES

FROM.................................

LINES AND FILL IN THE ADDRESS.

N.B.—IF ADDRESSEE CANNOT BE FOUND, will the Company Commander kindly see that this book is *NOT* returned to Sender, but handed to the addressee's companions to read.—Editor, UNION JACK.

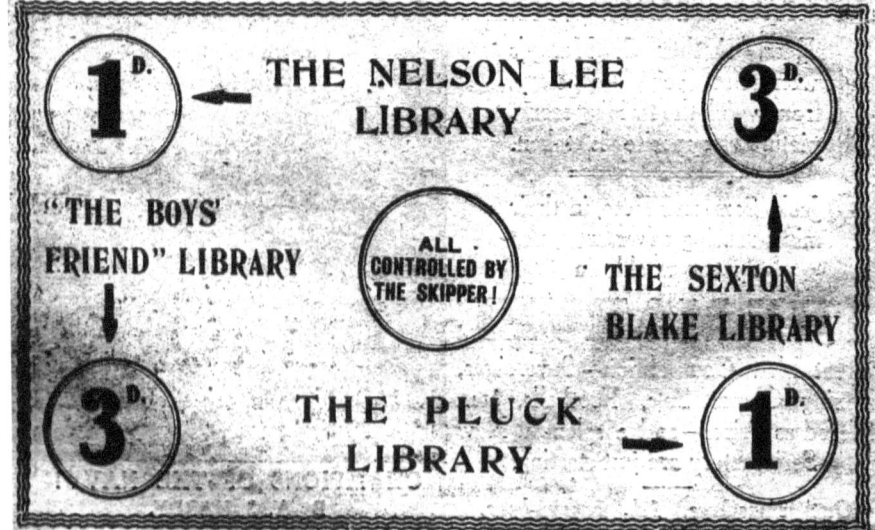

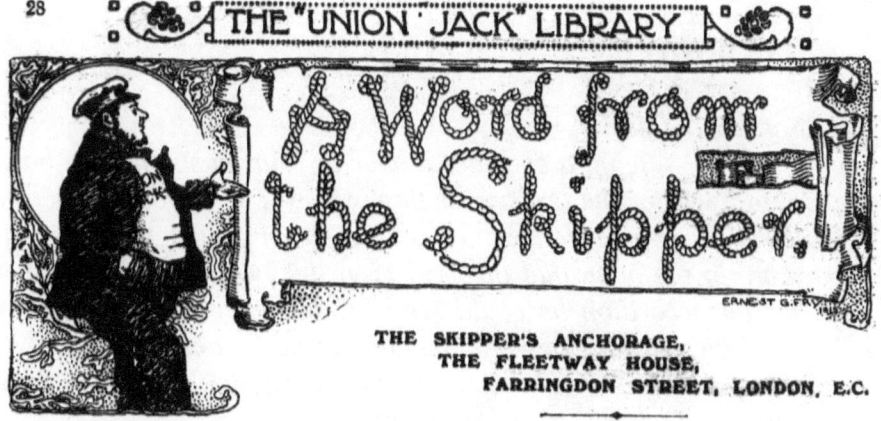

THE "UNION JACK" LIBRARY

THE SKIPPER'S ANCHORAGE,
THE FLEETWAY HOUSE,
FARRINGDON STREET, LONDON, E.C.

A WORD ABOUT THE SOLDIERS' LETTERS.

I am more than pleased, my chums, with the manner in which you have been responding to the soldiers' appeals in the Union Jack. This week, in answer to one letter, I had seventeen offers of help. Naturally, only one out of these was accorded the honour. I want the other sixteen to remember that although their offers were not taken advantage of, they were none the less appreciated. Now, this week I have published some more letters—only about a tenth of the total amount I have received from the Front—and they are a fairly descriptive set, inasmuch as they voice the requirements of most of the other letters in hand.

So, when in sending for one of the addresses on this page, my chums, you may receive an entirely different address. In this event I want you to understand that it is another soldier who wants the same article, or a similar article, as the article on this page. Do not forget that I have in hand any number of letters asking for articles of clothing, musical instruments, and so on, which are naturally crowded out of the Chat page. Therefore, should any of you possess a little article that you do not require, even though such an article has not been asked for on this page, send along to me and ask me whether I think the article will be needed. If it is, my chums, you may be quite sure that I shall send off the address right away.

Let me here take the opportunity of voicing the thanks expressed in my letters from our boys at the Front. One and all concur in the statement that Union Jack readers are the best of the lot.

ACCORDION.

"PRIVATE F. HENNAH, No. 3715,

"*Saffron Walden.*

"*Dear Sir,—Being a constant reader of your most valuable book the* **Union Jack** *for the last two or three years, I hope you will not be offended if I appeal to you on behalf of my comrades for an accordion, in the hope that this will meet the eye of a fellow-reader who has an accordion he could send us. You may be sure that my chums and myself will extend to him our warmest thanks.*

"*Thanking you in anticipation, and wishing the* **Union Jack** *every success, I am, sir, yours faithfully,*

"PRIVATE F. HENNAH."

BOXING-GLOVES WANTED.

"PRIVATE R. E. OWEN,

"*Chwilog, S.O.*

"*Dear Sir,—Seeing that I am a constant reader of your most valuable book, I am hoping you will not be offended of me asking you to send me a set of boxing-gloves. I would be very much obliged if you could let me have a set.—I am, yours sincerely,* Private R. E. Owen."

"PRIVATE E. EIGINBOTHAM,

"*B.E.F.*

"*Dear Sir,—Being a reader of your paper for a matter of about five or six years, and having same sent out to me every week, I beg to ask if you could supply us with a set of boxing-gloves, as we have often tried to arrange contests in the section, and we have always been held up for the want of gloves. We are in billets at the present time, and the dark evenings hang heavy on our hands. We are not particular about the set being secondhand, and I sincerely hope you will try and oblige us. The majority of the men have been out since September, 1914, and they would be greatly pleased if you could do this for us. In our section at the present time we have one or two decent boxers, and it seems a pity that these men should not have the opportunity of training. We have very few opportunities of sport here; as we have little or no athletic articles of any description.*

"*Trusting you will not be offended at me asking for the gloves, I*

100

remain, yours sincerely,
   E. Higinbotham,"

FLUTE OR BRASS WHISTLE.
"PRIVATE F. J. PEARCE,
"*B.E.F.*

"*Dear Skipper,—By being a constant reader of your weekly paper the* **Union Jack,** *I notice you have been kind enough to obtain various instruments for troops at the Front, so I take this opportunity of asking if you could get me either a flute or a brass whistle, to enable me to cheer my comrades during the winter months. Any other small instrument would be very acceptable, so that we can form a small band and have impromptu concerts.*

"*I might mention I am always anxious should my parcels get lost, and I should as a consequence miss my weekly read of the 'U. J.' The yarns are very good and exciting, and, as far as I have seen, very extensively enjoyed out here. I myself always pass mine on to my chums when I have finished, which no doubt will ensure further constant readers after the war is over.*

"*Wishing you and all your readers the best of luck in the New Year and a Merry Christmas, I remain, yours truly,*
   "F. J, PEARCE."

FROM A PRISONER OF WAR IN GERMANY.
"PRIVATE F. W. WARNER,
"*Deutschland.*

"*Dear Sir,—I am writing on behalf of my comrades and myself to see if you would publish this in your paper, the dear old 'U. J.,' for some of the readers of same, to send us a few old 'U. J.'s to read. Most of us read them here. The great fault is, we cannot get them. I have been able to get two in six months, so you see how we are placed. If none of your readers are able to send them, would you mind sending us a few? Well, I must close now, as your time is precious.*

"*Wishing you and your valuable paper the best of luck and success, I remain, yours sincerely,*
   "PRIVATE F. W. WARNER."

THE SKIPPER.

Printed and published weekly by the Proprietors at The Fleetway House, Farringden Street, London, England, Subscription 7s. per annum

Agents for Australia: Gordon & Gotch, Melbourne, Sydney, Adelaide, Brisbane; and Wellington, N.Z. South Africa: The Central News Agency, Ltd., Cape Town and Johannesburg, Saturday, January 8th, 1916.